Vacation with Three Boys

ROYAL HAREM
BOOK TWO

LEXIE MIERS

CHAPTER 1

Henryk

What had been meant to be a short vacation for one turned into a week-long vacation for four, plus one snarky security person who was at present seated across from me reading a newspaper, something he seldom did in my presence.

The mechanics of being on vacation weren't the kind of details I troubled myself with. I had people who arranged all the details of my travels. They saw to the fact that I had top security, privacy, and arranged my calendar. This was not that kind of trip.

This was not a matter of State or a duty I was performing for the crown.

This was a vacation. And although we traveled by royal jet for privacy, we were booked into a very public resort. That had worried me every day since we got here.

As though he could read my thoughts, Raymond looked up from his daily dose of news, folded it in half, and slapped it onto his lap as if he thought I needed the interruption.

"You're not acting like you're on much of a vacation, sir," Ray said from where he was seated on a couch much too short for his long legs. My private security guard was tall and built like an oak tree. Women loved him, even after they found out he was gay. He was mysterious, like some sort of covert spy, with his fancy clothes and ridiculously expensive shoes.

The hotel suite was large, with four large bedrooms and a common area, an office and a full bar. Room service was twenty-four hours a day and we had a private patio, a hot tub and an infinity pool. Somehow, both managed to be the perfect temperature no matter what time of day or night. This place was opulent and luxurious, fit for a king. Or a crown prince, anyway. I was quite comfortable here, even if I hadn't been able to leave my work behind. Fortunately, the room was equipped with various pieces of technology, including a video phone system.

And come to think of it... I glanced at Ray. "Did you book this room for us before or after I agreed to come along?"

He smiled. "Why does that matter?"

Ray anticipated my movements often before I even knew my own wishes. He shook his head when I didn't answer. "It doesn't matter. You're here in a room that fits *your needs*."

I shook my head and went back to working because I needed to get some things accomplished. He could play his games another time.

But he wasn't finished talking. "Sir, the American photographer, Harlow, is here."

Every once in a while, Ray managed to surprise me. This was one of those moments.

I looked up from my computer screen once more. "Here in this room or here in Ibiza?"

I smiled as calmly as possible because obviously she wasn't in this room, and because if I allowed it, my emotions—mostly driven by anger—would take over.

Harlow had been following my family since I was a boy. Back then, it was my family who provided the stories—both true and untrue—but that didn't matter to Harlow. Since then, she'd moved on to me, and I was featured in her magazine more often than not.

"At the resort, sir."

He didn't have to care, and obviously didn't. But the PR team and my government would kill me if I disgraced or let anyone else disgrace the crown.

"I checked. She seems to be on vacation."

Sure, she is.

Until I happened to step out of the safety of my room. "As soon as she knows I'm here, it's over. If she gets a whiff of my cologne, she'll start hunting... find out about Erin and make me out to be the worst sort of royal."

I was well aware that my arrangement with Erin, Silas, and Viktor was non-traditional. I didn't need it splashed across the tabloids for public dissection and discussion. And my parents certainly wouldn't appreciate it, either.

In fact, my mother would be livid. And disappointed. I wasn't sure which was less ideal.

Ray shook his head, frustration burning in his sharp gaze. "You know I love you, Henryk."

His frankness put me immediately on guard. He was using our friendship now to keep me from lashing out at him, which I'd never done and probably never would, for whatever he was about to say.

"I don't care how important you are or think you are. If I'm on vacation, not even a picture of a prince skinny dipping in the Spanish sea–"

"I don't skinny dip."

Raymond shook his head again, faster this time, probably driven by the confusion mirrored on his face. "That is beside the point."

"I have a very sensible pair of shorts for swimming." I knew precisely his point, but I had jokes too.

"Sir..."

I pretended not to hear him, and held back a laugh. "They have blue triangles." I pretended to ponder with a squint and tapped my chin with my finger.

"Henryk."

"No. They're red triangles."

His eyes flashed. "Henryk."

"Oh, for God's sake, Raymond. I get the point. You think she won't care. You think it's a coincidence that we're here at the same time." He was incredible at his job precisely because he trusted no one, so his faith in this tabloid writer was out of character.

"Henryk, you are at a resort in Spain. Relax. Enjoy. Have fun." His smile transformed into a smirk. "If you think she's going to let you have it any other way, you're more naive than I thought."

Ray was as much friend as personal security, but I was still the crown prince. "Watch yourself, Raymond."

He shook his head and stood. "No, my prince." He stared down at me. "As usual, I will be watching you."

When he walked out, I considered all he'd said. I would've loved to have been so carefree and enjoy my time with the trio unhindered by worry. But he was right. If this was my last chance to enjoy my life, I was blowing it. Not that he'd said that in so many words, but Raymond rarely said what he meant in the exact words he meant them.

Aside from that day in the playground in America where I'd met Erin all those years ago, I rarely let go. This was an opportunity. And if this was truly the last one I was to have, I shouldn't waste it.

But before I could even let that sink in, my cell rang and my mother's coronation picture as she'd stood by my father appeared on the screen. This was going to be bad.

Of course, it was going to be bad. It was my mother. I couldn't remember a time that she'd ever called me for a reason other than to complain, usually about my brother, something he'd done, and how I'd failed to train him to be a better prince.

"Mother." I felt my whole body stiffen as I spoke. I was always on guard when I spoke to her.

"Henryk!" Her voice was already an octave higher than normal, which meant she was agitated. "I sent Marguerite to your room this morning so that we could begin the wedding preparations, and you were not there."

I hadn't been there for three days already. "Yes?" I knew very well what she wanted me to admit, but I wasn't in the mood to be chastised. "Mother, I will be back by the beginning of next week. Then we can all sit down together and make plans for a wedding that is being forced on me like we're living in medieval England." I wasted no opportunity to gripe about my forced nuptials, but I rarely complained to my mother about it. Usually, Raymond bore the brunt of listening to my ranting.

"You were born the first son of a king. You don't have the

same luxuries as your brother." She sighed. "Posy is a lovely girl, and you could come to love her."

"Yes, I'm sure you think so." This marriage had been arranged when I was born, but I hadn't known about it when I was seven and accidentally married three other people.

"All of a sudden, I don't know you," my mother chastised. "You've always been the one to uphold the standards of your family. To follow your father's wishes." Instead of asking me why I'd chosen now to turn on them, she just stopped speaking.

I assumed that meant it was my turn. "Before, my *father* never forced me into a marriage I didn't want."

She sighed, loud and long, the sigh of a woman who wanted me to hear her disgust and disappointment. "You'll be king. You will need a queen who can stand by your side, who knows the behavior expected by the court and your peers, the council, society." She'd lowered her voice to the *do as I say and don't embarrass me* hiss that was her normal way of speaking with Nickolai.

"Yes, I'm well aware of all that." Of course, I was. I'd been hearing it since my childhood.

"Then what is the purpose of all this incessant complaining? You'll do as you're told by your father and king." She raised her volume as if she could use my fear of her—which had faded long ago—to inspire me to behave in the way she wanted.

There was no amount of complaining that would change her mind. "I will be home by the beginning of the week."

"Yes, see that you are, or I will command Raymond to drag you back home in chains if that is what it takes." Duty and honor above all.

"I'm sure you will." Of that, I had no doubt.

"Henryk, this match with Posy is for the good of Lichtenstein.

For the people. It will provide stability for both countries. An alliance that neither side would be inclined to break, and we would honor in times of peace, and, heaven forbid, war. She's a pretty girl. You'll make beautiful children." And there it was. Her real reason. She wanted grandchildren. The next generation of royal offspring to strengthen the alliances of my country.

I didn't like it, but there was nothing I could do about a tradition that had lasted through the ages. "I know, Mother."

"Then stop complaining. You have *five* days." She stressed five as if I was unsure of the progression of days remaining until the beginning of the week. "Make your memories or whatever this unplanned and unsanctioned trip is about, then get home and do your duty."

My mother was the queen of our country and our family. Crossing her was treason. Even I wasn't immune, as she so often reminded me.

"Yes, Mother. I'll see you then." I hung up. She'd made threats previously, and she probably wouldn't follow through if I went against her.

But when it came to this marriage, I was pretty sure I'd see a totally different side of her.

CHAPTER 2

Erin

By the time I returned from sightseeing with Silas and Viktor, I was famished and dying to see Henryk. He'd stayed behind to "work," but I suspected the truth was that he hadn't come along because he didn't want to be seen in public with us.

I didn't know if he thought one of us would get carried away with the PDA or if he was just overly cautious. I suspected it was a mixture of both.

He'd done so well the first two days we were here. He'd gone to the beach with us, frolicked for about an hour, then stayed in a cabana tent while the rest of us tried to convince him to come out.

But at least he hadn't been as insistent on staying in the room as he was today.

I couldn't really blame him for wanting to stay in his room, though. This place was super swanky. He'd booked out an entire suite for the four of us, and his room was the largest and nicest.

In the two nights we'd been here so far, we'd not really taken advantage of the pool or the hot tub, but I hoped tonight would different. With regard to that, anyway.

Silas sat beside Viktor on one sofa in the common area, and I sat beside Henryk on the other.

I laid my hand on his shoulder. "How was your day?" I scooted closer because I liked the scent of him. I also wanted to do more than hold his shoulder, so I ran my hand down his back.

"It was a day like most others." He didn't sound overly bitter that he'd been left out of our adventures, but the upbeat tone didn't compensate for the look on his face.

This was not good mood Henryk.

More than anything, I wanted to change that. I wanted to see his smile.

"Well, we're back now."

I smiled when he nodded. "I can see that."

I took it as a good sign that he didn't break the gaze we were locked into. I could see the passion in the depths of his eyes that I'd witnessed the other night. I wanted another taste of it.

But before I could lean forward and kiss him, my stomach growled, reminding me that we'd come back here to eat. "Should we order room service for dinner, or would you like to go out?"

If he wouldn't go out to sightsee with us, the chances of convincing him to leave the hotel were paper thin. I understood that he'd probably seen Ibiza before, so the thrill wouldn't be the same for him as it was for us, people who had only been out of the United States once.

He twisted suddenly towards me, and I lifted my arm to rest on his shoulder while my fingers toyed with the hair at the nape of his neck. Facing me, he was so handsome it took my breath away for a full second.

Then a slow smile spread across his face. "You are very radiant today."

That in no way answered my question, but I wasn't unhappy to hear it.

"Thank you." I couldn't look away from him. I was captured in his potent gaze that hinted at desire. I was here for it. "Now about dinner…" I had no excuse for why I changed the subject just then. I wasn't starving to death.

But all I could think of was getting to the next part of the day. I'd had a very nice time with Silas and Viktor and the sooner we got dinner out of the way, the sooner I could have an even better night with all three of them.

And there wasn't much in life I wanted more than that.

Henryk glanced away, and the loss of that contact hit me like a sucker punch to the stomach. But then he said, "Tonight, we can eat in, enjoy the hot tub and the pool, and maybe tomorrow we can all take a trip."

When he looked back at me, there was a glimmer of something that hadn't been there before. Like maybe he was going to fulfill his end of this vacation with us without me having to remind him that he'd agreed to stay and enjoy it fully.

Whatever he had planned for tomorrow was fine by me, but the use of the word "maybe" made it seem like Henryk was going to try to figure out an excuse to stay in tomorrow. I would deal with that when it happened. There was no reason to make it an issue before it became one.

Plus, a little hot tub time with my prince and my house flippers was just what I needed after a day of walking the streets of

Ibiza. Not that I was complaining. My sore muscles and aching feet were well worth it. This was a once in a lifetime experience.

Silas grinned at me. "I've been wanting to try out the hot tub. Looks awesome."

Viktor nodded. "Oh, yeah. Let's do it. A night of relaxation sounds like a plan."

We'd spent the day drinking fine wine, eating our fill of aromatic and spicy food, and when we'd finished lunch and needed to walk off some carbs, we'd seen an old cathedral and browsed at a street market.

I'd never learned Spanish, but Silas was fluent, and he translated for Viktor and me. He told us about the history of the cathedral and helped us at the market as we asked about items or talked to vendors.

The day had been peaceful and comfortable, but I'd missed Henryk.

Henryk got up and walked over to the hotel phone and ordered our dinner in Spanish. He was so eloquent and when he spoke the language, it sounded natural and beautiful. When he hung up, he smiled at the three of us. "Shall we sit in the hot tub while we wait for dinner?"

That was an idea I could fully get behind. "Definitely," I said. He didn't have to ask me twice.

"Sounds good to me," said Silas, as he and Viktor headed off to their room.

I gave Henryk one more grin before I turned on the ball of my foot and ran back to my bedroom. I retrieved a previously unworn swimsuit from my luggage and slipped into it. The white bikini deepened my leftover summer tan, and I appreciated the way Silas smiled and then bit his lower lip when I walked out.

He was the first of them ready, and as he strode towards me in nothing but a pair of swimming trunks, my breath caught in my throat.

"You look fucking hot, Erin," he growled at me, reaching out to grab me by the waist and haul me up against his huge body.

I'd pulled my hair into a high ponytail but left it swinging down my back. Silas slipped his hands between my hair and my skin, making me shiver.

His touch was electric, and his breath came in a low hiss. "Your skin is..." He broke off and dropped his head and pressed a kiss to my collarbone. My hands slid up his muscled arms and clung to his shoulders.

His lips were full and warm against my skin, and I wanted so much more. I went up on my tip toes to kiss him but was surprised when he pulled away and laced his fingers in mine.

"Spa time," he announced as he tugged me gently towards the hot tub. Steam rose off the hot water and bubbled away, smelling clean and slightly salty.

I stepped in and sighed as the hot water wrapped around my leg. "Oh, yeah. That feels awesome." I dropped down into the water and moaned at the wonderful feelings swamping my body.

When Henryk and Viktor came out of their individual rooms, I couldn't help the smile that lifted my lips. There was nothing quite like the sight of all that raw and blatant masculinity.

Coming for *me.*

My hormones began to bubble right along with the hot tub. Tonight was the night we were all going to finally be together, I could tell. And I wanted it to be so special.

I slid back into one of the four corners of the spa, with Silas in the corner next to me. I gazed up at him, feeling like the luckiest girl in the world.

"I loved seeing Ibiza with you." His voice was a low purr and it vibrated inside my soul. He brushed his finger down the side of my face when I turned to look at him.

"And I loved seeing it with you." Being with Silas was easy. He didn't expect me to be a certain way or demand I act according to a set of rules he had for me. He was also stunning to look at. They all were. His hair was shorter and a little less blond than when we were kids, but when he smiled, he was the same boy I remembered.

"Where did you learn to speak Spanish?" I asked, deciding to jump to a safe subject so I didn't jump on him. But then my hormones overpowered my brain cells. "It's sounds so sexy when you speak it."

He grinned at me, then said, "*Quiero besarte hasta que enloquezcas de pasión y necesites hacer el amor conmigo.*"

I didn't know what he'd just said, but I certainly liked the way he said it. "What does that mean?"

He pulled his lower lip in again and half-smiled. "It means I want to kiss you until you're mad with desire and you need to make love with me."

"Oh." A wave of warmth swept over me that had nothing to do with the hot tub water. "We should do that."

He grinned and slid his arm around me, then pulled me in for a kiss.

The moment his lips touched mine, I was lost. When his tongue swept inside my mouth, I gasped then slid my hands up to caress his face. I wanted to be closer to him. I needed him to be deep inside me.

His hand slipped into the cup of my bikini top and toyed with my nipple. Zings of pleasure made me arch into his palm, and I plunged my fingers into his hair, deepening our kiss.

There was something about kissing a man with full lips and a soft mouth. Viktor joined us in the hot tub, and he grabbed me around the waist and turned me so I was straddling Silas while Viktor reached inside the front of my bottoms. When Viktor's finger brushed my clit, I moaned into Silas's mouth.

We continued kissing until Silas untied the top of my bikini and pulled it down so my breasts were bare. I leaned back into Viktor's chest and gasped at the onslaught of attention I was getting.

Viktor turned my head towards him and kissed me as Silas flicked my nipple back and forth with his tongue. When Viktor bent to suck the other nipple, I was on fire with need and desire pooled in my belly.

The warm water bubbled against my skin, and I was lost in a sea of pleasure. Then Henryk joined us in the water, and I had to go to him. I reached out my arms and suddenly it was his mouth on mine, his tongue dueling and dancing inside my mouth.

I couldn't stop the moans and gasps that echoed in my throat. I was being pleasured from all sides. Silas and Viktor continued sucking and nibbling on my nipples, and Viktor's fingers circled my aching clit.

I broke Henryk's kiss to sob, "Oh my God."

I wanted more. I wanted everything. One inside me. One in my mouth and one licking my clit. Oh... fucking hell. The thought of that was so intoxicating enough that I moaned loudly and tried moving my hips, hoping Viktor would slide a finger or two inside me.

Henryk pulled my face back to him and deepened the kiss and tightened his hand in my hair. The slight tug combined with the light nibbling on my nipples made me cry out. I couldn't help it. This was fucking incredible.

I pulled out of the kiss once more so that I could look up at Henryk. Viktor's fingers continued caressing me, driving me insane. I took Henryk's hand, slid two fingers into my mouth and sucked for a few seconds then pulled them into the water and around my backside. "Finger me. Please. I'm dying."

Henryk dragged his fingers down my ass to my pussy then pushed inside. I cried out as he quenched that ache but made me hungrier at the same time. He moved his fingers inside me, and his thumb gently pressured my ass.

My mind was screaming, and my body was liquid. Silas and Viktor continued tongue-massaging my nipples while Viktor played with my clit and Henryk fingered and kissed me.

Oh, God. This was the best foreplay I'd ever experienced, and I'd never been happier to be a woman.

I wanted to ask them to stop so we could go inside and finish this somewhere more private, but I couldn't do more than moan and writhe against them. My body clenched tightly as desire coiled in my belly and twisted into pure, white-hot pleasure.

My back arched higher as my pussy tightened around Henryk's fingers. My body bucked, completely out of my control now and I cried out, a moan that split the evening apart echoing in my ears.

My orgasm came at me in rolling waves. My body convulsed and jerked until the pleasure finally ebbed and flowed away. I fell against Silas's chest, languid and pliant.

"Let's go inside," Henryk said, his voice gravelly as he pulled his fingers from my body and slipped out of the tub.

Viktor stood up in the hot tub and held his hand out for me. Despite my lethargy, I managed to get to my feet on wobbly legs and step out of the spa.

I held Viktor's hand as we followed Henryk into his bedroom. I stepped out of my bottoms then unfastened the top altogether and let it fall to the floor.

I knew the exact choreography that I wanted after dreaming about it for days. I crawled onto the mattress at the closest edge then moved so I was on my knees.

I reached for Henryk and pulled him down for a kiss. He'd dispensed with his shorts sometime between the hot tub and his room. His dick was already hard and ready for me, and damn, was it beautiful. Long, thick and perfect.

I wrapped my hand around his shaft for a moment, just to feel his heat against my skin. Then I said, "Lie down on your back."

It felt a bit strange to tell a man who was going to be king one day what to do, but he didn't even pause. He got into place, flat on his back on the bed. I straddled him reverse cowgirl style, holding onto his cock before sliding down on top of him.

I couldn't stop the groan that was pulled from my mouth as he filled me. I pulled his arms around my body so that he could play with my nipples.

The effect of him beneath me was enough to elicit a soft, "Oh my God," before I glanced at Silas. "I want to take turns sucking you and Viktor while you take turns eating my pussy." I'd never been so bold or brazen with a man–and certainly never *men*–before.

But in this moment, I needed to fulfil a fantasy and they were letting me have all the power. That in itself was the biggest turn on.

Silas and Viktor glanced at each other, big grins on their faces. Then Viktor said, "Hell, yes."

I took Viktor into my mouth first while Silas went down to lick my clit. I couldn't not watch so I sat up enough to take Viktor into my mouth and also stare down while Silas flicked his tongue across my clit. He held my gaze as I grinded up the length of Henryk's cock then back down. Behind me, Henryk moaned then sat up enough that his mouth was beside my ear.

"I love watching you slide his cock in and out of your mouth while I fuck you."

His words almost made me come right then and there. I loved that my prince liked to talk dirty.

Henryk continued, "And when Silas put his tongue in your pussy with my cock, or his tongue touches my dick when I slide it out, it makes me want to explode inside of you."

Oh, God. This man certainly painted a picture with his words. He gave my nipples a couple firm twists and I sucked in a breath then moaned it out.

"You like that?" He did it again and this time I arched, pulling Viktor's cock deeper into my throat.

Viktor laced his hand into my hair and held my head. "Oh, yeah, Erin. That's so good."

Silas shifted and started stroking his cock. I wanted to watch, but more, I needed to *feel*, to make Viktor come, to hold it together until I could suck Silas, too. And I was spiraling fast. Henryk's cock was a masterpiece, and his words were driving me mad.

I concentrated on everything going on around me, sucking

harder until Viktor's balls tightened, and he groaned as he came. I swirled his dick with my tongue and swallowed every last drop of his salty cum.

Then he pulled out and traded places with Silas.

Silas was thick and long, and I pulled him in with a deep, hard suck and he cried out, grunting. His hips moved in the same rhythm I was using to suck. And then I couldn't hold back anymore. All of this was too much for me to resist and I blew apart, harder, hotter than the last time.

As I bucked on top of Henryk's perfect cock, Viktor moved, and Henryk curled his fingers into my hips and bounced me up and down on his cock. With every thrust, he made my orgasm last longer and longer.

I kept sucking Silas until with one more thrust into my mouth, he came too.

Henryk's breath was at the back of my neck. "You ready, Erin? I'm going to come inside you."

His words made me shudder with longing, renewing the fire within me. He cried out and his body went stiff as he wrapped his arms around me and pushed deeper.

When he came, the hot pulses within me made my entire body spasm. I drank him in, tears leaking down the side of my face as my heart cracked open.

I'd always enjoyed sex, but this was a whole other level that I'd never experienced before. There had never been anything in the world like it.

Somebody needed to say a prayer, because I didn't know how much my heart would be able to take kind of sex. This was the Brad Pitt, a Ferrari, the World Series and Super Bowl in one day of sex.

Henryk pulled me down onto the bed with him and the room was filled with the sounds of our labored breathing. Silas and Viktor joined us on the huge bed and as I drifted off into the most blissful sleep of my life, I found myself wishing that tomorrow we could do it all again.

W hen we were all buckled into seats facing one another toward the back of the semi-empty shuttle from the resort, Henryk heaved out a breath. "I know you all think I'm being difficult, but my parents are not the forgiving type. So, any escapade that is discovered by them will lead me into a dark family situation."

Henryk was wearing a semi-cool disguise thanks to Erin. She'd painted a star in glitter eyeshadow around one of his eyes, slicked his hair back with gel and put him in one of her t-shirts. It was super tight and stretched across his chest so the world could see his nipples, and a pair of skinny jeans.

He looked nothing like the prince I'd first met.

Blah. Blah. Blah. We'd heard it all before. "We know. Future king. Country at stake. Gotcha." I didn't mean to be an asshole even though it kind of sounded like I did. I tried to soften the words with a nod and finger guns. Honestly, it was like I was off my meds, but Erin smiled.

He nodded. "Raymond can attest to my mother's almost constant state of worry about the appearances of things. About duty and honor."

I glanced at Raymond. "Don't look at me, Cinderella," he told the prince.

Erin leaned in and dropped her hand so that it laid over his. Then he turned his hand and interlinked their fingers. Everything looked very easy between them. Natural. And I wondered how they'd slipped into that kind of relationship. Why she'd bonded in that way with him, and not Viktor or me.

Not that it mattered, we were all together. But I wondered if she had to choose, would she choose him? Would she choose at all?

My plan was never to make her choose. Not for more than a few hours, anyway.

The shuttle bus pulled up to the front door of a dance club, so we climbed out and walked in. Not like a prince with two guys and a girl, but like three guys who couldn't stop following their girl.

There was a cover charge and Raymond handled it for all of us. Then, because she was Erin, she dragged him–Raymond–out to the dance floor. The music was loud– Electronic Dance Music– and it wasn't really my style. But the vibe in the air was contagious and eventually we were all dancing on Erin's portion of the floor. Raymond left us to go to the bar, and returned with shots in test tubes.

It wasn't ten minutes later that a woman came charging toward the prince. Raymond used his big body to block her, though she continued calling out, "Prince Henryk! Prince Henryk!"

Too quickly, and just when the drinks were starting to do their job, Raymond ushered Prince Fancy Pants out of the club.

I rolled my eyes towards Erin, who was worriedly looking after the fast-disappearing pair. "Uh... so, are we staying to dance? Or..."

"I think we should go too." Erin said, already edging towards the door. "If Henryk can't stay, then we should go home too."

Erin rushed out after him and Viktor stuffed his hands in his jeans and shuffled after her.

I sighed and ran my hands through my hair. This was not how Erin had wanted the night to go. And although I understood that Henryk had to leave, we certainly didn't have to.

I begrudgingly followed them outside and waited at the curb, shielding the prince from anyone's sight until Raymond could secure us a ride back to the resort. Of course, by the time the shuttle bus returned, a crowd led by its boisterous ringleader–the woman who'd discovered Henryk inside–had come out and was trying to get through us to get to him.

They were mostly drunk so there wasn't much fight to be had, but it was clear that now that he'd been discovered, the only place we could go and be assured of his privacy was back to our accommodations.

As we climbed into the bus, I looked at Viktor. He wore his annoyance like a mask, with narrowed eyes and a grim line to his lips. I nudged him, trying to lift the mood even though I was annoyed myself. "It's all good. We have a private hot tub and a swimming pool at the resort. Nothing like a middle of the night skinny dip."

He shrugged. "I liked the club."

Henryk looked at us as we took our seats. "I apologize."

I nodded. It really wasn't his fault, and I didn't want our

mood to ruin the night. After all, our nights were numbered and counting down. "No big deal. We'll just switch the party to the suite."

And we would, because we were in a package deal situation. For Erin, anyway. And probably for each of us. Viktor would figure it out eventually and be fine with it. On a regular day, he didn't have a jealous bone, or even an angry one. This wasn't a regular day.

I watched Erin beside Henryk. She was beautiful. Kind. Doing everything she could do to ease Henryk's guilt for making us leave the club.

She said, "It doesn't matter, you know. We'll still have a good time. No one blames you."

Well, aside from Viktor, she was right. But he would come around.

By the time the bus dropped us off in front of the hotel, Viktor was already in better spirits. Mostly. There was an errant grumble about using the front door if we didn't want anyone to know he was here, but other than that, Viktor remained mostly silent.

Erin was giddy enough for all of us. She giggled when she stumbled, and Henryk had to catch her to keep her from planting herself face first into the carpet. She chuckled when he stood her against the wall, and she pulled me in for a kiss. She laughed when she hopped into Viktor's arms and told him, "Drive Miss Daisy home!"

He ran her inside the suite past Raymond, Henryk, and me.

Raymond saluted us. "I'll retire to my room. Call me if you need me."

I turned back to Erin, watching her as she flung her clothes off as they made their way through to the patio. A shoe zinged past my head and the other sailed toward Henryk. Then her top landed on the lamp and her bra found the sofa.

Fatigue hit me hard and I settled onto one of the chaise lounges. It had over-stuffed cushions that felt like clouds when I reclined back into it.

Viktor shook his head as Erin dove into the pool, naked and glorious now. "I'm going to bed." He went inside his room and shut the door.

I stared after him. Seriously? He left the party? Why? I shook my head and turned back to the main show.

Erin pouted, then wagged her finger at Fancy Pants as he shook his head at her.

"Come on, Henryk," she begged. "Come swim with me."

"It's late."

"You ignored me all day." She puffed her lip out again. "Please?"

A simple *please* was all it took to talk him out of his fancy pants and his too tight t-shirt. Once he was naked, he dove in, and she clapped her hands. When he surfaced, Erin was waiting for him and pulled him into her for a kiss.

It was one of those searing kisses that looked every bit as hot as it probably was. Her fingers raked through his hair and then she curled her arms around his neck.

When we'd been in poly relationships in the past, I'd watched Viktor with our woman, and he'd watched me. There was some thrill in a live action porn show, and my dick stirred at the picture they made.

Henryk lifted Erin out of the water, and she giggled happily when he climbed onto the deck after her. Then he lifted her to her feet, swung her up into his arms, and carried her to the chaise.

That chaise was near enough to mine I could see the action very well, but far enough I couldn't reach to touch her.

He set her down on the cushion on her back, then held himself over her, kissing her as water rolled from them onto the cushions. For a few more seconds they kissed, then he moved down her body to swirl his tongue around her nipple, blowing softly on it then moving to the other.

She turned her head then crooked her finger at me. "Come over and join us?"

"No, thanks," I said and smiled at her. "I wanna watch."

"Will you play with your cock for me?" She had a breathy little voice that made my dick swell almost painfully against the button fly of my jeans. I yanked it open, and my dick sprang free.

I curled my fingers around the shaft and gave a firm, hard pull. I couldn't stifle the groan that rose in my throat.

She kept her eyes on my cock and her hand in Henryk's hair.

"You like watching too, Erin?"

She nodded. "I love watching you." Her back arched and she came off the cushion, still holding Henryk's head so his mouth stayed on her nipple. "Do you want to watch Henryk fuck me?"

"Yes." Oh God, I wanted to watch that.

The prince groaned and shifted his body, moving like he was going to go down on her but knelt between her legs instead. He moved her legs apart until they were each hanging over the side of the chair then slid his fingers inside her.

She was spread open for him and touching her own nipples now. They were hard little points, and she was twisting and pinching. My mouth watered for a taste of her flesh, but I didn't move.

Tonight's fantasy–I wasn't sure if it was hers or mine–was to watch. I stroked my cock slowly, not wanting this to end anytime soon.

She lifted her hips and met the thrust of the prince's fingers, but she looked at me, watched my hand on my dick.

There was nothing fancy about jerking my cock while I watched the prince finger her, but it felt incredible. So fucking good, it wouldn't have taken much for me to come.

She glanced up at Henryk and smiled when he licked her juices off his fingers. He turned her over so that she had her ass in the air and her tits were hanging down. Oh, God. That position was my weakness.

As he slid into her from behind and groaned, the urgency of my stroking heightened. As Henryk's speed increased, so did mine. Erin raised up so that her back was flush against his front, and I couldn't stop watching them move together. The way they danced and thrust, the way her breasts bounced, and her mouth opened on a gasp.

It was beyond hot.

When she slid one hand down her belly and swiped her fingers over her clit, I almost came right there. Then she moved her hand down further and made her fingers into a V to rub against Henryk's cock on each side as he pushed in and out of her.

And best of all, she kept her gaze locked on mine. The intensity of that connection was just another layer of pleasure. This was so fucking sexy, I had to take my hand off my cock and let myself settle a moment before touching myself again. I didn't want to finish before they did.

Her body jerked again, and her face contorted into a mask of desire and need. "Watch me come, Silas. Come with me."

As if I could look away.

I watched Henryk power into her, watched her bounce on his cock, all the while stroking my shaft. "Fuck." This was almost as good as fucking her myself.

My balls tightened at the same time she cried out and clutched Henryk's ass behind her, holding him deep inside her.

"Oh, God, Henryk!" she shouted and it was enough to make me explode. I grunted and squeezed the head tight while cum shot from the tip of my dick. A second later, Henryk went full-on tense and gave a final thrust, held onto her hips, and groaned from somewhere just south of his soul.

I collapsed deeper into the cushions, enjoying the shivers of pleasure pulsing through my balls and over my body. Then, when I could finally move again, I picked up one of the folded towels beside the chair and cleaned myself off while Henryk and Erin panted together. She smiled at me and then turned her head to kiss him.

There was nothing about her that I didn't like. She was sensual and sexy, beautiful and sweet. This was the kind of a woman a man didn't let go of, even if he had to share. And I didn't mind one bit.

CHAPTER 4
Viktor

I was barely awake enough to remember where I was when my phone started pinging. I ignored it and headed to the bathroom for my morning piss, then a quick shower to wash last night's club off me. But finally, I picked it up.

Silas was a live-in-the-moment kind of guy. Never watched the news. Never cared about world events. Not that he was stupid. He preferred to read books to newspapers, listen to music rather than news reports. I, on the other hand, liked to keep up on current events. So, I generally awoke to headlines pinging across my screen.

I was in Spain, though, and I considered starting this day without a thought to TMZ or US World and Entertainment News. On the other hand... I swiped the screen, let it find my face, then read the headlines.

Uh-oh. Fancy Pants wasn't going to like this one bit. And the chances of him suffering a small stroke increased with every word I read and the pictures I saw that flashed onto the screen as I scrolled. *Oh, fuck.* His small stroke just became massive.

Drunken orgies and drug-fueled all-night parties–Prince Henryk's Ibiza holiday is a naughty one.

And there were somewhat blurred–but not enough for plausible deniability–full-color photos of the three of us in the hot tub fondling and kissing Erin. A picture of the prince in his "disguise" grinding against Erin in the club. A blown-up picture of a very naked prince with his dick about to poke into Erin on the chaise with Silas beside them holding his dick, undoubtedly ready to jerk off while he watched them fuck, which was his go-to when he was too tired to participate.

"Oh... fuck." This was bad, on about twenty-eight levels of suck.

The caption under the picture was at least somewhat complimentary. *Henryk's sizable package on display.* Use of the word sizable wouldn't be enough to stave off his aneurysm, though.

I walked out of my bedroom and saw Silas sitting at the table with a plate of eggs in front of him the size of a small city. "Good morning, buddy." He nodded to the table. "I called down for breakfast, and a few minutes ago they delivered all this." He laughed. "If I had this kind of pull, I would be so fat. And happy."

There were trays and pans of food set up, lining the center of the table. Eggs, bacon, sausage, fresh fruit. We had it all. But instead of getting into the gluttony of it all, I handed him my phone.

He read for a few seconds, scrolled, brought the phone closer then pushed it out farther, then pinched and pulled the screen. He looked up at me. "I've heard that the camera adds ten pounds, but does it add inches too?" He handed the phone back. "Instead of Fancy Pants, maybe we should be calling him Anaconda."

"Save the jokes, Garden Snake. He's going to see this shit." As if we'd summoned him, Henryk opened the bedroom door and walked out. His hair was tousled, and he was wearing jeans and a t-shirt, which was unusual.

Amazingly, he looked mostly normal instead of like a prince trying to fit in. I shoved my phone into my pocket, a certain amount of guilt for badgering him to come along sliding through my veins.

"Good morning." I didn't look at him. Couldn't. Not because of the Anaconda thing, but because I didn't want to ruin his last few minutes before he discovered what had been printed about him. I was afraid that if I so much as glanced at him, I was going to blurt out the whole damned thing, headlines and all.

And before any of us did that, I probably needed to call Ray in. I'd never had to deal with an irate prince before and didn't know if there was a certain protocol to be followed.

I glanced at Silas, who had suddenly developed a keen and intensely focused interest on his scrambled eggs. He mumbled a greeting and shoveled in another bite, looking everywhere but at Henryk. If Henryk noticed, he didn't mention it. Instead, he simply sat down at the table and poured himself a glass of orange juice. He probably needed to rehydrate after last night. But I sure as fuck wasn't going to mention that.

And then Erin walked out, also from Henryk's bedroom. She looked at me and I glanced away. It would've been too easy to tell her.

Then she looked at Silas. He didn't bother to gaze up from his plate. "What happened? What's going on?" Her words came quickly and at a slightly heightened pitch. But her brow was pinched, and she was staring at me.

Then the prince looked at me too, and I crumbled under the

pressure. I would be the worst criminal on the planet. I would rat myself out to the cops as soon as they said my name.

But I really didn't want to be the one who brought this up.

"Um... shit." I nodded towards Silas. He looked at Erin, then at Henryk, then shook his head at me.

"Seriously, what's going on?" Erin demanded with hands on her hips.

I glanced at Silas. "Coward."

He shrugged and I pulled my phone out, opened the news app and handed it to Henryk.

To his credit, the prince waited until he handed my phone off to Erin before he lost his shit.

"Fuck! How the fuck am I supposed to explain this to my parliament? To my fucking mother?" His accent didn't do much to soften the sounds. Although cursing his way sounded proper— a bit more regal than when Silas or I did it.

He pulled out his own phone. "Do you know that I have a person in my employ who does nothing but search my name all day long to make sure the news is flattering? That I haven't upset the world with some off-handed remark or some slight gesture?" He looked at his screen then turns it toward us. "My cock is a fucking meme."

Oh, the clever people in the world.

Silas looked up. "At least they won't be able to say it's small."

Henryk shot Silas a glare that would've melted a lesser man. This guy was going to be a kick-ass king.

Henryk turned away then back again. "My mother is going to see this." He shook his head. "She sees every fucking thing. But at least my cock was my own. Until now. Until you blackmailed me into coming on this wretched vacation!"

Erin's mouth dropped open as Henryk stormed into his bedroom and slammed the door. He'd hurt her and if he wasn't dealing with a very public shit storm, I would've marched into that bedroom and beat his ass all around it.

"Hey." I moved closer to Erin and used my finger to tip her chin up. "He didn't mean it. He's just... pissed off."

"Blaming me." She closed her eyes then opened them and looked away.

"No, he blames us. It wasn't your fault."

"Those are my tits that look like cow udders hanging down. My ass in the air." She picked up my phone again and looked at the picture again. "Fuck. My parents are going to see this."

Yeah. This might've been paradise, but there was a spy, someone watching us, apparently. I took the phone from Erin and stared at the picture of us in the hot tub. Only Henryk's face was visible, and the shot seemed to have been taken from above. I went out to the patio to the hot tub and looked up. There was nothing to stop anyone from seeing into the fenced and gated patio if they were on the roof.

We would have to be careful. Obviously, they'd paid someone at the club for the picture. And then I glanced at the last photo. It was taken at an angle from the direction of the beach, but still over the fence.

Something was rotten in Ibiza.

When I walked back inside, I sat at the table. No way could we figure out how to help our prince if we were operating on empty stomachs. And he certainly belonged to all of us now. I made a plate and watched Erin nibble on a bite of Silas's toast. Even watching her eat was an experience. At seven years old, I'd obviously had impeccable taste in women.

"What can we do for Henryk?" Silas asked, one plate polished off and another busy being filled.

"I don't know." She shook her head. "He's a prince. I don't know the rules for his... reign?"

Silas sat back in his chair, pushing his fork through his scrambled eggs. The guy could eat a boatload of those damned things. "Honestly, is it really a big deal? So, the world got a little look-see at his dick. Which photographed really well." He shrugged like a prince's dick pic wasn't big news. "Soon as Captain America sends another naughty tweet or some other celebrity couple puts their torrid little divorce action on TV, nobody is going to care that a prince from some tiny European country got his knob polished while I watched." He might not have said it with a snooty accent, but he had a point. Today's scandal was forgotten tomorrow, unless he happened to be a British prince. Which he wasn't.

Erin dropped her head to her hands. "I should go talk to him." But she didn't get up. She stayed and heavily sighed instead.

What could one say in this situation? Back home, no one cared what Silas or I did. We could get by with sharing women, or even trading women when the women were into that. But this was quite different.

Neither of us were princes. No one followed us around looking to embarrass us with pictures of us partying and getting laid.

"You should eat something and give him a minute to work out whatever he's got going on in his head." Last thing he needed was the reminder of this fuck up, walking into his room like sex on a stick and trying to console him.

And she looked certainly doable. Like a walking billboard for doable. Her tank top was a perfect pink that complimented her skin tone and stretched across her chest, highlighting the curve of her breasts. Her white linen shorts left a lot of luscious leg exposed, and my dick tightened because of just seeing that much of her bare.

I wanted run my tongue along that smooth silky skin and...

I shook off the thought and refocused on the matter at hand. She didn't need to go in and see Henryk when he was still so unhinged about all this.

"Yeah." Silas laid his hand over hers. He was the more affectionate, touchy-feely one of us. "Let him process all this. He's embarrassed, and rightly so. And he probably needs to wrap his head around it."

My lips twitched and a chuckle escaped. "God knows there's enough of it."

Silas grinned. Even Erin smiled.

That's when Henryk walked out, just in time to catch us all laughing at his dilemma.

He shook his head. "I'm glad you all think this is so fucking amusing."

"We don't, Henryk." Erin's voice was soft. She'd probably be able to get by with laughing. Silas and I might not be so lucky.

Silas nodded. "We just don't think it's the end of the fucking world."

Erin stood and walked toward him. When he held up his hand to stop her, she changed direction and walked onto the patio. This was not a good moment to be vacationing with a prince in Ibiza. Not while there were people watching us.

CHAPTER 5

Erin

I knew that this wasn't a problem that Silas and Viktor particularly cared about. They were playing video games on the console attached to the big screen. And by big screen, I meant it was half the wall. At least eighty or eighty-five inches of television. They were playing some shooting game and the noise was deafening.

I walked out to the patio again. Henryk still hadn't come out from his bedroom and these two had told me that it would be better to not bust in there and try to make him see that this wasn't a big deal. I wasn't going to do that. I'd only been concerned with offering him support, something it didn't seem he got a lot of.

Instead, I paced. Planned. Worried.

I was deciding on the best revenge to take against whatever smarmy little reporter had decided to photograph such an intimate moment, then zoomed in to splash it across the front page of the virtual equivalent to a newspaper.

I didn't care who saw it. I wasn't ashamed of my relationship with Henryk. And I'd never been what anyone would call conventional. I was just a girl getting through my life. What people thought about me wasn't my business. Much the same that what I thought about them wasn't their business. For the most part, I strived to believe that with my whole heart.

But I wasn't naïve enough to think that they wouldn't judge. And Henryk would pay the price for that. It wasn't his fault. He'd been taught all his life that what other people thought mattered, that he had a certain standard to live up to and foursomes probably didn't fit that standard. Although, whoever decided had obviously never benefitted from having one.

I smiled at the thought. These last few days had been incredible. Definite *Dear Diary* days. I hated the person who ruined it, who tarnished our vacation. It wouldn't have taken much to convince me to hunt them down.

The by-line was a single name–Harlow–but in one of Henryk's outbursts, he'd called Harlow *her*. Cher. Madonna. Harlow. All one-name wonders. But only one of them was trying to take down someone I cared out.

I grunted in frustration and watched the water roll into the beach.

"Hey."

I looked up as Ray walked onto the patio and came to the rail on the beach side. I walked up to him and asked, "How is he?"

"He's furious, as expected." Ray shrugged and sighed. "This is going to take a minute for him to work out."

A minute was probably too optimistic.

I nodded. "What can we do? There has to be a way we can help him." I couldn't just let him take the fall for what we'd all decided on, what we'd all enjoyed. I couldn't let them punish him for living his life.

Ray looked at me for a few long seconds. They felt long, anyway.

"I know Henryk. The anger we saw today is a good sign. On a normal day, he's reticent. Holds it all inside. Barely human." Ray had worked for Henryk for years, apparently. "He's never had to deal with scandal before because he keeps his nose clean. But the king and queen are used to this kind of thing. Many articles have been written about them. Some true, some not."

I didn't know their history. Hell, I'd never even known Lichtenstein was a place. And I never read those magazines. Ever.

"So, what do I do?" I glanced at Ray.

"Hang in there. Give him some time to work it all out in head." Not that I had much choice about that. I sure as hell wasn't going in there. This was at least twenty-five percent my fault. Probably more.

Ray continued, "Henryk's younger brother, Nickolai, has been kicked out of three prep schools and been cited multiple times for underage drinking. The family is used to dealing with antics."

"But not from Henryk." Stating the obvious was one of my special skills.

"No. And that's what makes this such fodder for the masses." If Ray said so, there wasn't a reason to doubt him. He knew Henryk better than anyone. And if he said Henryk only needed time, I believed him.

I glanced towards the entrance to the hotel. "Maybe I should go talk to the front desk. Henryk's privacy at this very expensive and supposedly exclusive resort has been compromised. I bet they wouldn't like their customers to know–"

"You mean go to the front desk and validate the story so that some desk clerk who's going to be identified only as a source inside the hotel, can claim their five minutes of fame by portraying you as irate" –he used air quotes– "and frantic? So they can say the woman from the photos has been identified and has gone to fight for the embattled prince? That's what you want to do?" He cocked an eyebrow and when he put it that way, the idea sounded bad to me too. "Don't be naïve, Erin."

"Fine, what do I do?" I wasn't mad at Ray, although I probably could've softened my tone of voice. I hated that this relationship –if that was what it was– was hurting Henryk.

"Keep your heads down. Let it die down on its own." Now he sounded like every adult I'd ever met as a kid when the bullying had been big and bad. But I didn't come to Ibiza to keep my head down and stay in the hotel. I was going to figure this out.

Before I made any headway in that direction, my phone rang in my pocket and I pulled it out and looked at the screen. It was work.

"I'll leave you to it," Ray said and walked back into the suite.

I contemplated not answering, but I couldn't keep living on Fantasy Island. Eventually, I was going to have to go back home, and I couldn't afford to make an enemy of the man who controlled when and if I worked.

I slid my finger across the screen. "Hello."

"Erin. Hello. I hope you're enjoying your vacation." He could say whatever he wanted, but Joffrey Vandeloo of Vandeloo and Associates cared about nothing but making money.

"I am. Thank you." The pause on the line was unnaturally

long. Surely, he hadn't called just to ask if I was having fun on a vacation he'd tried to deny me. "What can I do for you, Mr. Vandeloo?"

He chuckled but it sounded thin and fake. "Oh, please, call me Joff. Everyone does."

Not anyone I worked with. We had a few other names for him, and none were workplace appropriate.

"I'm calling because the Martin Quinn Gallery in Seattle has hired us to work on a campaign. They want print and visual media, radio, social media. They want the whole nine." He paused. "Yards. I mean yards."

"Yeah. I got that." Joff was an over-explainer, or a mansplainer as he was much less than affectionately known. "I'm on vacation."

He cleared his throat. "Yes, yes, I'm aware. But they have champagne taste on a beer budget."

I waited, sensing a backhanded compliment coming. Or maybe just an outright insult. With Joffrey, one never really knew which way he would go to be nasty. "And?"

"And you're my most talented junior associate. I thought if you would like to take point on this, it could lead to larger accounts." There had to be a catch. I waited but he didn't continue. "Erin? Are you still on the line?"

"Yes." And there was no catch.

"I would need you to start working immediately. We have a meeting with the client on Wednesday of next week, so we'll need to go over the pitch on Monday. I'm out of town on Tuesday. You can pick your team—one from graphics, one from copy—but this will be your account."

Wow. This was a great offer. My own team. Taking point. These were dream phrases.

I'd been lucky to land a job at Vandeloo right out of college that wasn't just about getting coffee and letting him play grab ass. I'd been the personal assistant of the other Vandeloo, Joffrey's younger sister, Helena, and she recommended me for a junior associate position.

But the timeline was the problem. "I'm out of town until Saturday."

He sighed. "I suppose I can ask Martin Pollard, but Helena speaks so highly of your skills and your ambition, I thought—"

"No, no. Don't give it to Martin." I wanted this. Had dreamed of it, a thousand or so times. I didn't know when I would get another chance like this, and I didn't want to turn it down. "Can I have a day to think about it?" It was a lot to think about. It was three days. I had three days to decide what I was going to do.

"Noon tomorrow." Then he hung up.

I imagined Joffrey ended all his calls in some form of this fashion, but never with a goodbye. He had such an overinflated sense of self that he probably considered himself too important for a traditional "Goodbye".

I set the phone beside me on the chaise and stared at it. I didn't want to let Helena down after she'd gone to Joffrey and sung my praises enough that he decided to give me my first account. But I also wanted to see where everything with Henryk, Silas, and Viktor was going. And that kind of opportunity–the one with the guys–might not happen a second time.

CHAPTER 6

Henryk

My mother seldom raised her voice, rather she practiced the art of controlled rage. But today, she was loud. "I have no words."

I remained calm because one did not yell at his mother, especially when she was also his queen. "It sounds to me as if you have plenty of words, Mother." She'd been cursing and berating me for the better part of twenty minutes. She started with, "What in the absolute hell were you thinking?" and moved onto, "How fucking dare you disgrace this family, this country?!"

It wasn't as though I'd planned any of it. If I was anyone other than a prince, who I slept with would be of no concern to anyone. That, however, wasn't logic enough to convince my mother, because it was my unfortunate luck to have been born a prince. I'd never thought of it that way before. Never considered myself anything but privileged.

But so much of this week-long vacation had been a revelation to me.

"Even Nicky doesn't humiliate us with such antics."

I tried not to roll my eyes and failed miserably. My mother had spent most of my childhood comparing me to my British cousins. Which was fine, at the time. But using my little brother–he was barely eighteen and had, much to my mother's shame, a Canadian girlfriend–to shame me, was out of line.

Nicky had made a mockery of his education, his family name, his upbringing while I'd been dutiful and obedient. A shining example of how a royal son should act.

"Oh, please, Mother. Antics?" It was one of her favorite words with regard to my brother. There he was, *pulling more of his antics*. I'd heard her say it a thousand times. She'd asked me more than once to talk to him, but Nicky was just struggling to find himself.

Being a normal teenager was difficult enough. Being the second born and with newspapers following him around and stories being written made it worse. Unfortunately, he also had friends who had no problem videoing his bad behavior and posting them on Instagram. Nicky's issues were a bit more complex than the average teenager.

"Antics, Henryk. I thought you were better than this. And what are they going to say about you?"

I shook my head at her even though she couldn't see it. And it was probably a good thing, too. Nothing infuriated my mother quite like anything she perceived as insolence. And mine, while it would have been a first, would have probably sent her careening over the edge.

"What happens if this... woman gets pregnant. Can you imagine what will be reported then?" She huffed out an exasperated sigh. "Your child would be next in line to inherit the throne and there would be a shadow over his head. A blight. And it would be due to your inappropriate behavior."

Leave it to my mother to bring my unborn children into the conversation.

"Mother, you do not have to worry about children." And even if she did, I wasn't admitting anything else to her.

"So you're using condoms? Does one of the others put it on for you?"

"Now you're being crude." And it was unbecoming on about a thousand or so levels.

She scoffed. "I guess we're both trying new things." Mother was nothing if not clever.

"I can't unwrite the article. What do you want me to do?" I sighed because as soon as I said it, I knew the very thing my mother—my queen—would demand of me.

"I want you to come home, show the world, who's now watching you, that you are every bit the prince we've raised you to be and that this..." She paused and I knew the next word wasn't going to be a fun one. "*Dalliance* is nothing more than a mistake." She paused. "For heaven's sake, Henryk. Women on the television are talking about the size of your... organ."

I wanted to shout at her, to tell her that this was more than a *dalliance,* but I couldn't. She was right. I'd shamed my crown. Shamed my country. Behaved with a total disregard for all the things she and my father held in the highest esteem–grace, respectfulness, heroism. They'd raised me to be someone who was worthy of being respected and admired, adored, honored.

Even so... "For God's sake, Mother. It's a penis."

"Your father is beside himself." She scoffed again. "He can't even speak about this. And the royal press is having a very difficult time, so I've made the appropriate excuses about why your *penis* would be front page news."

"And what might those be?" There was no telling what excuses had been made on my behalf. Of course, there would be no truth telling–that I was a man with varied interests.

"Drunkenness, for one thing. Sowing your wild oats before your pending marriage, for another." She sighed. "Your father couldn't even speak to King Harold."

That was my Morovian bride's father.

"It's good that he has you to speak for him then." And not for the first time, I wished I could be anyone other than who I was. I hadn't intentionally disgraced my family. I'd simply done one thing in my life that wasn't about who I was, but rather what I wanted. And if they gave me another chance, I planned to do it again before I went home and stepped into the role of Posy's husband.

I groaned. It was involuntary, but the thought of giving up Erin for Posy made my stomach ache.

"You will be home by Monday," she said, then hung up.

I tossed the phone onto the bed as the door opened and Raymond walked in. "Is there anything I can do for you, your highness?"

The situation was obviously dire enough for him to call me something other than Henryk. Not a good sign.

"Yes, you can insist my mother make my brother the heir so I can have a life of my own." Now that I'd had a taste of this kind of freedom, of this sort of passion, of Erin, I didn't want to go back to Lichtenstein. Certainly not without her. Maybe not at all.

He nodded, though there wasn't a smile in sight. "It's going to blow over. Just hang in there, Henryk."

Blow over? Hang in there? "Have you been reading bumper stickers again, Raymond?"

He was probably right though. And I believed that right up to the moment my phone rang, and Posy's photo flashed onto the screen. I held it up so Raymond could see. "Oh, God."

And I had no choice but to answer as Raymond walked back out of the room. "Hello, Posy."

"How could you?"

If ever a man could hear the intent of murder in a woman's voice, this would've been what it sounded like. Deep, precise, each word bitten but forceful. And I had no answer for her, none that would calm her anyway, so I said nothing.

"I am completely humiliated!" I was still without words, so there was another pause. "Say something, dammit!"

I sighed but quietly so as not to make this worse for either of us. "What should I say, Posy? That I'm sorry for what happened? I'm not. That I'm sorry it was reported? That wasn't my fault. That I'm sorry you found out and got hurt?" Hurt might not have been accurate. "I am."

Maybe it was my tone or the fact that I was in fact sorry she was hurt, but she changed her approach. "I don't understand why you have this need..."

It wasn't for her to understand or try to dissect.

"But you are humiliating me in front of the world, and I won't have it. I demand you end this right now!" Shrill was the new tone.

And this was to be my life until I died.

"You demand? Or what? You won't marry me? Fine. Don't marry me." Wouldn't that solve my problems. I should've been telling her to be reasonable, that as soon as we were married, this would stop. But I didn't, because I didn't want to marry her and more, I hoped she used this as a reason not to.

"You don't want me to be your queen?" Now she was playing the victim. I couldn't tell if the crack in her voice was real or put on for sympathy, but this time my sigh was loud. "That's it, isn't it? You like *her*."

I didn't answer because the only suitably truthful reply would hurt her. And I wasn't prepared to lie. She would be able to tell.

While I didn't want to marry her, I wasn't intentionally going to put her down.

Unfortunately, silence, too, was the wrong answer. She shrieked in my ear, "I want you back at the palace now! Do you hear me, Henryk? Today!" Then she slammed the phone down into its cradle. She'd probably called me on a landline just so she could do just that. There wasn't anything satisfying about hanging up on a person on a cell phone.

I understood Posy's humiliation, although it wasn't *her* erection posted on every form of media available because *she* let *them* talk her into climbing into a hot tub naked. Because *she* had the audacity to have sex with a beautiful woman during what was to be a private vacation on what was also to be an equally private patio.

The door opened, and instead of Raymond, it was Erin. She shut it behind her and stood with her back against the wood. I tried for a smile but the best I could hope for at this point was that my grimace didn't scare her away.

"Can we talk for a minute?"

By this time, even though I had searched, I hadn't found an expression that looked bad on her. I needed a reason not to want to throw her onto my bed and kiss her until we were both burning with need. And she wasn't really providing one.

Instead of speaking—I didn't really trust myself—I nodded.

Maybe I should've been mad at her for convincing me to do this, the vacation, the group sex. But I couldn't be mad. And I'd tried. But I'd never experienced anything so incredible in my life as this vacation. And if all I was meant to have were the memories of what we'd shared, then so be it.

These were the kind of memories that would see me through the rest of my dutiful life. And damned if I wanted to cut them short.

She looked at me, every bit as beautiful as any dream woman I'd ever thought of. "I'm sorry this has been so traumatic for you. It wasn't supposed to be."

I nodded because she was right and sincere. But still, this was a private thing, and it had become international gossip fodder. It was unfair and damning. "We just wanted you to have a good time too. Especially since you paid for everything."

"I know." Their intent didn't really matter. The only intent that mattered was the media, and their intent was to ruin my life, obviously.

"And there are way worse stories out there."

Of course, there were. But none with my name on them. And right now, that mattered to me. But of all the people in the world, Erin was the last one I wanted to look like a fool in front of. And I couldn't explain this to her without sounding over-inflated and self-important. "I know."

"You're a single prince who had a party. Is it so bad, really?" Her voice was soft, and she made me want to be the kind of guy who didn't care what others thought of him.

But I'd never even talked out of turn in school. This was a full-blown scandal. I wasn't adept at dealing with anything like this.

"According to my mother and Posy…" I nodded. "So very bad." Of course, my mother and likely Posy had the uncanny ability to turn any event, good or bad, into a tragedy.

"Well." She grinned, shrugged, played it like this was no big deal. "You deserve a little wildness before you settle down to marriage and forced family."

I couldn't have agreed more. But my entire life was circling the drain and the hope that the whole thing would blow over wasn't especially helpful. I needed a solution, not playing card affirmations.

But as unhappy as I was in that moment, as upset as my life had become, my body reacted when she walked closer. When she sat beside me. When she cupped my face in her palm and turned me toward her, I couldn't stay mad. Even if she'd been laughing or poking fun, her touch was a balm.

"I know this is bad." She tilted her head.

"Not so bad," I managed to whisper back, and in this moment, it wasn't.

Her touch, her being here made it bearable. Probably more than simply bearable, but pretending it hadn't happened wasn't a solution. It wouldn't calm my mother or soothe Posy. Stop her from playing woman scorned on a world stage.

The universe I was carrying was heavier than it had ever been. And of all the things I wanted to say to Erin, I couldn't say any of them until the chaos died. And only God himself knew when that might occur, if ever.

CHAPTER 7

Silas.

Viktor's pacing wasn't entirely annoying. He did it to think. To work shit out in his head. Apparently, for him, there was a correlation between feet moving and brain working.

On a normal day, I ignored him. It was easy on a *normal day* because he wasn't huffing and puffing like he was about to blow a house down. Today, though, the Big Bad Wolf vibe was strong with him. It was fine, considering everything that was happening, but it was growing tiresome.

I tried to ignore him, to concentrate on the game on the big screen—Xbox, not football— but the noisy breathing was distracting.

Instead of throttling him, I set the controller on the sofa beside me and looked up at him. "This is helping you? Really?"

He shot me a glare. "Is she going to stay in there all day?"

I shrugged. Technically, the time element mattered since we only had a couple days left, but our opinions weren't likely to get her out of there faster. "I don't know the protocol for interrupting a royal hissy fit, but I guess we could go in. Though, if he yells *off with their heads*, you're on your own."

Viktor and I had been friends for years. We worked together, played together, drank together, shared women, and now we could add vacationed together to our list. I'd been on the receiving end of more than one *go to hell* look, and he had taken a few drunken "go fuck yourself" rants from me. In the end though, we figured our shit out.

He plopped into one of the armchairs, leaned back and stared at the ceiling. "I didn't come here to watch pretty boy pout over some stupid fucking article."

"Pictures, too." To be fair. And they were explicit.

"It's not like the headline read *Prince's Pitiful Package*."

"Or *Prince's Half Karat Family Jewels*." I chuckled, feeling clever.

"Oh, shit." The door to Fancy Pants' room was behind me. And apparently too silent to hear open.

I twisted as Erin walked out and stood behind the prince. She was wearing a scowl—beautiful as it was—and the prince scoffed at us. "If you call the tabloids, I'm sure they would happily pay you for your first-hand account. Although, I hope you'll paint me in a better light than *half karat*."

I cleared my throat and faced my embarrassment head on. "Sorry. We were just... sorry."

The prince poured himself a drink. I looked at Erin. Her lips were parted, and if not for the narrowed eyes, she might've looked flirty.

Viktor, though, looked at the prince. "Everything isn't a tragedy. You could tell them all to go get fucked." He chuckled more to himself, and I knew it was about to get ugly. I'd seen him like this one other time and that night had ended in a fist fight and a night in jail. "I'm betting they probably need it as bad as you did."

It was probably his tone that Henryk took exception to. Probably the fact that Viktor was mocking him as much as everyone in his world who had a less than positive outlook on today's news cycle. And it must've been a slow day because the prince had taken top billing and there were pictures of the resort, of us going into the club, coming out, dashing into the bus, the pics of our hot tub time. Everything we had done in and outside the club with the prince had been documented and photographed.

It was little wonder he was a basket case. The headlines weren't kind. I'd never read the sort of papers that published shit like this. I didn't care who Brad Pitt dated or about Tom Cruise's religious preferences.

I just couldn't understand exactly why he was acting like this was the worst thing that could happen to a person when clearly, it was not. Lichtenstein was a wealthy country, and he was a wealthy prince.

There was a whole world out there beneath his station in life and he needed to recognize it.

"Look, *Fancy Pants.*" This time I said it with attitude. I didn't care that it was probably as insulting to him as *dumbass* would've been to me. I just wanted to knock him off his high horse. "This isn't a problem. Homelessness is a problem. Not having enough to eat is a problem. A flattering picture of your dick in a newspaper is not a problem." I shook my head. "And it certainly isn't a tragedy."

"You wouldn't understand." He dismissed me with a wave of his hand.

I cocked my head at the pompous prick. "Because I'm just a construction worker?"

He shot me a look. "Frankly, yes."

"*Really*." The arrogance in this guy was a whole vibe. And I didn't care who he was or how big his crown. "Do you hear yourself?"

He looked me up and down. "Of course."

Anyone else might've thought for a second, reconsidered the attitude, but not this guy. And like he was made of steel, he walked closer until we were almost nose to nose.

"You really think you're big enough to start something?" The threat wasn't an implication. It was a statement. This little fuck better back off or he was going to learn really quickly how tiny he was. I lifted eighty-pound bags of concrete mix on a regular basis.

"Big enough to finish it."

From behind me, Erin said, "Oh my God, you guys. Either get out the tape measures or put them away because this is stupid." She walked around and pushed her way between us. "This is supposed to be a vacation."

Fancy Pants stepped back. And like she hadn't realized how mad she really was, she shook her head, breath hissing out of her like she'd sprung a leak. Then she turned and walked off to her bedroom.

Viktor shook his head also, but he was smiling, and followed her towards her bedroom and into the hallway. The door closed behind them, leaving me alone with Fancy Pants.

He looked at me. "Great."

I crossed my arms over my chest. "You can blame yourself for that one, princess. If you would stop whining about the papers following you around and writing about you and just let go and have a good time, she wouldn't have gone off with Viktor." I couldn't believe he cared so much what people thought of him. "Who gives a shit what they write?"

"I don't have any choice. I have to care."

His self-importance was staggering. "It's a gossip paper. The world doesn't care who you're sleeping with."

"Oh, you know so much." He sighed. "It's a lot easier to go into a peace summit or negotiate for my country when my pictures of my dick and what I was doing with it haven't gone viral."

Okay. He had a valid point. "Doesn't your country have a herd of snobby lawyers to sue the people who printed the pictures, with enough power to get them off the internet?" If it was such a big deal, there had to be some legal recourse.

"The tabloid is American and American tabloids hide behind your Constitution and the First Amendment to print their poison. They aren't held to any standard because it infringes on their rights." He sounded bitter, and I wasn't sure I could blame him.

"That's an argument for another day." I wasn't the one who was suffering, thanks to someone else's freedom of speech, so I wasn't the one who would be weighing in. "The point is, either figure out a way to deal with it or get over it. Making everyone else miserable while you mope and complain isn't going to serve you or anyone else you agreed to vacation with." I didn't want to come out flat and tell him that he was the one making it so much worse than it was.

For a few seconds he stared, nostrils flaring, breathing hard, lips compressed into a tight line. Then he nodded. "I know. It's just a lot to take in."

"Yeah." I could give him that. "You know what I do when shit is too real?" He shook his head and stared.

"I blow it up." I nodded to the television. "It's therapeutic." I handed him a controller, showed him how to use it and then watched him go.

I didn't know what classes they taught at prince school, or wherever he'd gone for his education, but this guy was a master strategist. I was glad he was on my team.

We played Xbox for a couple hours. Shamefully, there were high fives, fist bumps, possibly initiated by me. I had no excuse, either. It was just nice to not be at each other's throat.

When Viktor and Erin returned to the room, Henryk was standing up to get us a couple fresh beers. They served American beer in the bar and room service delivered but no one stayed in the suite to open them for us. So, we'd worked out a system. Last one finished had to get next round and since princes were taught to savor, Henryk was pretty much always the one getting the next round.

Erin cocked one of her pretty, arched brows at me. "All made up?"

"I shouldn't have made fun." I shrugged.

"And I have to lighten up. Not everything is tragic." Henryk looked at me and I nodded.

We'd worked it out.

CHAPTER 8

Erin

"This is a vacation! And you guys seriously want to do is sit in this room and play war games?" I looked at the three of them, and they all looked at the television.

While we were waiting for Henryk and Silas to work out their issues, Viktor and I had a couple of drinks and now I wanted to play. I might've been a little spoiled by all their attention but being ignored now didn't do much for my morale.

At the very least, the one who wasn't playing could've paid some attention to me, but they were all engrossed. And I had to take action. I didn't have a choice.

The minibar was stocked, and it wasn't really mini. We had pint bottles of liquor—whiskey, vodka, tequila, gin, even vermouth. Beer—American and several other varieties I didn't recognize. We had ice and various glass types. I picked up the tequila and walked to the sofa where Silas and Henryk were currently battling animated bad guys.

The graphics were amazing. I could admit that. And watching

the functionality of the game was interesting, the way they could zoom in and back out, split the screen, hunt and fight together was all impressive, but it only took a few minutes to bore me.

So, I dropped my hand in Silas' lap and let my fingers do the walking. He looked at me for a quick second, then went back to the game.

Viktor sat on the floor near the edge of the sofa and I glanced at him. He was watching the screen so intently I could've walked out naked, and they wouldn't have cared. And that was a thought I was tipsy enough to run with.

I went into my bedroom, checked my suitcase for anything in the sexy and skimpy categories, and found silky cami/panty set. It was semi-sheer, filmy more than see-through, but I slipped it on and checked the mirror. It was either use this negligee to get their attention or engage them in a drinking game.

We could drink when Silas made the *pft* sound, or when Viktor rolled his eyes, or when Henryk sighed. But I wanted them to be lucid and able for our next sex session, and if this didn't get me some attention, a drinking game wouldn't help.

I tipped back my tequila bottle for a quick shot of courage, then walked out of the bedroom to stand in front of the television. I waited for them to look then let my head fall back as I tweaked my nipples.

For a second, Silas shifted to try to see around me before he suddenly focused on me, then put his controller down. Viktor stared, and Henryk smiled.

Someone said, "Holy shit," though I wasn't exactly sure who it was. Then Henryk stood up and stalked toward me like I was prey.

He grabbed me around the waist, dropped a kiss to my lips,

then pulled me toward his bedroom. His room was massive and mostly occupied by a bed that should have had its own zip code. I smiled, crooked my finger at Silas first, then Viktor, and could've melted when they followed us into the room.

Henryk kissed me first and lifted me onto the bed. He might've been a prince, might've lived a life of rich foods and lazy days—I didn't really know—but he was ripped. He had abs I wanted to trace with my tongue, biceps that made a girl—this one, anyway—feel safe, protected, even. And for not being a guy who worked construction and lifted heavy tools and lumber all day, his body was toned and tan as if he did.

I lifted his shirt because I wanted to press my hands to the acres of smooth skin and rock-hard muscle. I wanted to do it right now.

He yanked his shirt off and over his head then looked at me, eyes bright with anticipation or desire. Maybe a mixture of both. It didn't matter so long as he didn't stop gazing at me. If he ever looked at anyone else this way, it would probably kill me.

He slid onto the bed beside me on the right side while Silas lay on the other. Silas kissed me while Henryk fondled my breasts and Viktor ran the tip of one finger in slow, lazy circles over my thigh.

Then Henryk turned my face towards him and kissed me deeply. Viktor leaned over me to slide his hands up my ribcage while Silas brushed his finger back and forth over my clit through the panties.

I gasped then moaned into Henryk's mouth, wriggling under their attentions. My fingers tangled in Henryk's hair as Silas slid his hand into my panties to touch me. My body was molten, my bones liquid. Every nerve was alive and thrumming under their touch.

Henryk continued kissing me, his tongue demanding against mine. I moaned softly when Silas pushed his finger inside me. I was wet and throbbing, so ready for them.

All of them. Right now.

Viktor held himself up on his hands and leaned forward to take one of my nipples into his mouth, swirling his tongue around the hard peak and making me arch my back for more.

Only my skin held me together when Henryk deepened the kiss. I could only hang on and hope I didn't melt away. When he pulled away, he stared down at me and said, "What do you want, Erin?" His voice was soft, but the intensity made my stomach flutter. I wanted everything.

"I want all of you." I couldn't have managed more words. And I didn't care how I had them.

With Silas on one side of me and Henryk on the other, both moved to completely undress. I would've watched intently because I loved to watch the reveal of muscle and cock, but Viktor lowered his head between my legs and kissed me. His lips pressed against my clit with such tenderness, I arched to meet him, my hips coming off the bed. When his tongue flicked out, teasing and caressing, I cried out.

Silas was undressed and back on the bed now, so I turned towards him, needing him. "I want to suck you." He brought his cock to my mouth with a grin on his gorgeous face. I gripped the base and swirled my tongue at the tip.

On the other side of me, Henryk knelt, and I wrapped the fingers of my free hand around his cock. When I turned my head toward him, I stroked Silas in time to what my mouth was doing to Henryk, then turned my head and switched back, all the while

Viktor continued licking and sucking my aching pussy, his fingers twisting in and out.

Life had never been so glorious.

I wanted it to go on forever.

My body tightened and desire pooled low in my belly. Henryk watched me as I sucked him and then his head fell back, and his eyelids fluttered closed. He was close, too. And I wanted to keep him as on the edge as I was.

I turned my head toward Silas, and he smiled down at me, moaning deep and long when I put him in my mouth. Then he gasped loudly when I groaned in pleasure so intensely, I could hardly concentrate on the matters in hand and mouth.

Henryk rubbed my breasts. "I want to be inside you, Erin." His voice was a raspy whisper and the sound sent shivers through me.

Viktor and Henryk changed places, so now Viktor was in my hand, long and thick and hard. Henryk was rolling a condom on. I couldn't see him, but I'd heard the wrapper and in my periphery could see his arms moving while I used my tongue to swirl the head of Silas's cock. This was the most exquisite and incredible experience of my life. This was better than fantasy, better than any reality I'd ever known.

Experiences like this were once in a lifetime. *They* were incredible. "Erin, wait." Silas pulled his cock out of my mouth, held it at the base then smiled down at me. "I need a second."

I turned to Viktor and when I took him into my mouth, his head pitched back, and he moaned. "Oh, God, Erin!"

Passion vibrated in my belly as Henryk slid into me, over and over again. Too soon, I was at the edge, ready to fall over.

Henryk held my gaze as I sucked Viktor. Desire rolled through me and every cell in my body tightened and coiled. He took my hips and pulled me in, then pushed me away and pulled me back again.

Viktor groaned again and withdrew, coming on my chest. A second later, Silas came and then Henryk reached down, touched a fingertip to my clit and I exploded. My body quaked and shuddered, shivered and trembled as I rode wave after wave of ecstasy.

Henryk tensed, then put his head back, thrust once more then groaned. He stayed still for long moments, allowing my orgasm to continue to squeeze him.

When I finally relaxed back, blissfully exhausted, he withdrew and went to the bathroom while I tried to catch a breath. Silas leaned forward and kissed me, and everything was perfect.

Never in my life had I felt so cherished, so cared for. It was intoxicating and I didn't know how I was going to go back to my real life after this. Or even if I would be able to. At some point in the next day or so, I had to make a decision about my future, but right now I only wanted to bask in the moment, to live this fantasy until it ended. I could feel our time together drawing to a close and I wanted to hang onto it, to not face the decisions that had to be made.

But real life was calling, waiting for us all and there wasn't one damned thing any of us could do about it.

CHAPTER 9

Henryk

I stood on the patio, listening to my father berate me over my cell phone. As soon as his name showed up on the screen, I'd walked outside and as far away from Erin and the guys as I could. They'd heard enough of my family's abuse already. The derogatory statements, the anger.

At least the sun was shining this afternoon and there was a light breeze rolling off the ocean. I wouldn't swelter and die out here while my father called me everything but my name.

"What in the hell were you thinking?" His voice was deep, angry, laced with the kind of judgment he usually reserved for Nicky.

"I was thinking I would live a little, have a bit of fun before I gave my life to the crown." I wasn't the first crown prince to sow a wild oat, and I certainly wouldn't be the last.

There was more than one crown in the world, more than one country with a monarchy. But it was a lonely job, solitary, and the time we spent serving the crown and our families and the people was all borrowed. I wanted to live my life while I had the chance.

"Live a little?" My father went from angry to irate in the turn of one phrase and it occurred to me that I should've let the damned call go to voicemail. I should've let my father vent to the little electronic voice that told him to say what he had to say and then hang up. "You're the crown prince of Lichtenstein. There is no opportunity you won't have, no life you won't be able to choose, but if you go on with this debauchery" –*hardly*– "I will petition the council to allow me to pass you over for your brother, Nickolai."

Wouldn't that be grand? An unreasonable response, though, was always my father's first go-to. And this time, I didn't care. "Go ahead. Trade me, the son who's given his life to this crown, who's never asked for anything for himself, for the one who has drank and fucked his way through Europe, across the United States, and into the Middle East." I never spoke to my king this way, my father. That was Nickolai's *modus operandi*. But I was too far in now to take it back. "Go ahead. See what your kingdom thinks of you then."

"And what do you think they are saying about you?"

I shook my head, uncaring. "Does it matter?"

His breath stuttered. "The monarchy is in a precarious position, and there are always those who want to see it fall. You know this." Of course, I did. They'd been preaching that exact line to me since I was a boy. "The council has mentioned taking it to the people, finding out if they would rather shift to a presidential rule of government, disbursing the family money to the people and the government. It's a Nicholas II situation here."

He was so dramatic. "You think they'll lock the family in a

basement and assassinate?" Of course, he did. Over the years, his paranoia had reached peak heights. And lately, the peaks stretched even higher. "For God's sake, Father, take a breath."

"Henryk! This is our history. Our future legacy, and you'll see it destroyed for what? Sex with an American woman who answers phones for a living? Is she worth taking down the history of your family, of your country?"

I had no doubt that if my father could have gotten his hands on me at that moment, he would've killed me. Had me locked up, at the very least. Especially once I answered the question.

"Yes. She's worth it." She was worth a crown, a title, a life I had strived my entire existence to be worthy of.

And that shut him up. He clicked off and ended the call. Undoubtedly, he would call back with more threats. Then, I would have to either stand my ground and resolve to never go home again, or I would have to turn tail and run back to them, where I would be forced to beg forgiveness in front of the court, in front of my father, and in front of the nation I was supposed to lead into the future.

I sighed so loudly my heart hurt. I should have thrown my cell onto the beach and prayed high tide would drag it out to sea, but I didn't. I would need it to make the appropriate arrangements no matter what I decided.

Or perhaps I was a coward. And everyone in this hotel, in this resort already knew I would be back at the palace on Monday morning, ready to make my apologies and my excuses and kiss ass until they forgot my dick had been front page news for a minute.

The waves rolled onto the beach, and I wondered if ever there was a time I would be unamused by such natural, beautiful things. A time that I wouldn't romanticize the crashing of the ocean into having a meaning more than its service to the moon.

"It's pretty, isn't it?" Erin's voice was soft behind me, her hand light on my shoulder.

I nodded. "When I was a boy and I came to the coast, any coast, I was enchanted by the sight of the rolling waves and the white foam. I thought it washed the world clean of all the bad. And that there was so much bad to clean that it had to come in and out over and over." I'd never told anyone those ridiculous notions before.

"The first time I ever saw the Pacific Ocean, I was terrified. It was beautiful of course, but we were on the cliffs and looking down. Below us the water was crashing into the rocks. It was so loud and violent. Dangerous." She turned me toward her. "Perception is subjective, Henryk."

I nodded. She was right. "But I have an entire nation to consider." I sounded pompous and grandiose, but I was honest about who I was and the reasons why I was this way.

"Who considers you, Henryk?" It was a good question, a fair question. And one without a good or fair answer.

"Kings don't have the same luxuries I have right now." And that was why I hadn't heeded my mother's demand to come home in that instant.

"So, are we just a minute of your life? Is this all ending on Sunday?"

I closed my eyes. Nothing in the world would've made me happier than staying here with her, with them. We were more than friends now, but I wasn't sure what we were exactly.

I shook my head because I didn't know the answer yet. "I wish I had a crystal ball, or some other way to know the future." There were no easy ways to get around all of this. "Whether I would be a good king, whether my brother could settle down and handle the job."

"You would give it up?" Her brow creased and her lips parted. This woman wore surprise as beautifully as she wore every other expression. "You would let him be king instead? Henryk, think of the good you could do. Think of the people you could help."

My country was wealthy, one of the richest in the world. She was right. If I were to be king, to accept the position for which I'd been training since I was born, I would have opportunities. Could provide opportunities to others.

She smiled up at me and the weight of the world on my shoulders eased enough I could see around it to the radiance inside her. She curled her arm around my neck and tugged me down for a kiss. "We both have decisions to make, things we need to be clear on. But you have to know that whatever you decide, I support you. I would hate to see you give up something that you don't have to, though."

Her voice was soft, but the words were the balm. "You'll be beside me?"

She pulled her lower lip between her teeth and turned her gaze down. "My boss offered me a job." She reluctantly dragged her gaze up to me. "It's what I went to school for, what I've always wanted to do."

"And you want to take it?" The ache in my chest spread and I rubbed a spot over my heart as if I could ease the pain with my own touch. I didn't want to think about what it meant.

"I don't know. I can't... not work. I don't have a country's riches." She didn't say it like a dig at me, but it was.

I frowned. "I would take care of you."

"While you're married to someone else." She shook her head and backed away from me. "I'm not that girl. Plus, this isn't about me, Henryk. This is about you. You're to be a king, and that is a responsibility you can't walk away from, but no one says you can't change what being a king means. No one says that you can't hang onto the pieces of yourself that you've found being here with us." And again, her smile lightened the tension furled inside of me.

I nodded and leaned in to kiss her cheek. This kiss wasn't about want or need, but about honest affection for a woman who made my every minute better. "I don't want to be without you, Erin."

I'd never been so honest with a woman in my life, never put myself out there like this for anyone.

She nodded but didn't say anything.

"I've never shirked responsibility before." I smiled even though it was the absolute last thing I felt like doing. "And I think it might break me to do it now."

She stepped forward once more and cupped my face with her hands. Then she slid her fingers into my hair and pulled me down so my forehead rested against hers. "If it does, if so much as one part of you chips away, I will find it and put you back together. I will not let being with me break you."

Every minute with her was more incredible than the last, and there was no way in hell was I ever going to let her get away. Even if she went back to her job, to her life and I took the throne that my father was almost ready to give me, I would make us work. No matter what I had to do or how I had to do it.

The rest of the night passed in quiet comfort. She was never out of reach, always beside me, close enough I could feel the heat from her body, smell the light and airy scent of her perfume.

She was everything I wanted in a woman. When she came to my room to sleep beside me, I held her and watched her breathe in and out, saw every smile as she dreamed. And even though I'd spent most of the night awake, when the sun was up and she turned to smile at me, I felt refreshed.

"Good morning." I leaned in and kissed her nose. She was a beauty at any hour, but now, with the softness of sleep still upon her, she was exquisite.

"Good morning." Her eyes were clear and bright, and she had the hint of a smile curved on her lips. "You're beautiful."

"I'm not beautiful." I was far from it.

She laid her hand on my cheek first. "You are here." And then slid it down to my chest to lay over my heart. "And most especially here."

She pressed a soft kiss to the spot, and I sighed at the easy affection between us. When she pulled back, she looked up at me and I began to roll her over so I could devour her.

But she stopped me as she looked at the table where her phone was vibrating across the surface.

She rolled her eyes as though exasperated by the thing, but when she checked the screen, she grinned, then answered. "Bree!" There was honest excitement in her tone. "How is everything?"

She listened for a moment then pulled the phone away and hit the speaker button. "Oh, for fuck's sake. On what site?"

After a moment, Bree sighed. "The fucking National Inquisitor."

Erin switched the screen of her phone to a browser then typed in the search engine.

A second later, she covered her mouth with her hand. "Oh,

fuck." She didn't speak again, but a tear rolled down her cheek as she showed me the screen.

The story wasn't about me or about my throne or the jeopardy I'd place on the monarchy. It was about her. Her life. Her past. Her relationships. And it insinuated that there were many men left in her wake. Some broken by her, some grateful to be away from her. It might've been fiction or the truth, and I didn't care, but this story came with photos too. Photos of her. Photos of me. Photos of us.

But worse than anything, it said that she was a witch of some sort that had undue influence on me, the crown prince of Lichtenstein. They painted her as some sort of threat to the throne. Someone wicked with evil intent who was leading me around by my cock.

I let my head fall back, tilted my chin up to look at the ceiling. Dragging me down was one thing. I was a public figure. But dragging her, making her cry, was something altogether different. I wasn't going to stand for it. I would never stand for it. And I was the only one who could fix this.

CHAPTER 10

Viktor

I'd never been a guy who cared what people thought of me. Take me or leave me, that was my motto. Your problem, not mine. Of course, I was well aware I wasn't everyone's cup of tea, and I wasn't going to be a best friend to the world. This wasn't new information to me.

Of course, it wasn't my name or my personal life being dragged around for the world, so I didn't judge Fancy Pants for his anger, or Erin for her utter devastation.

But there was a lot of cursing and crying going on in this moment. Erin stood up from the couch and shook her head, back to pacing in front of the television. "Who am I? Right? Who cares what I do?"

I shrugged and shook my head. "I don't... I don't know."

But I did. It was because she was the woman in the pictures with Fancy Pants. Some industrious little reporter—I was guessing it was Harlow—had gone all in to find out who she was. Found her hometown. Talked to people who knew Erin *way back in the day*.

And those people had been ready and willing to fill in details they claimed were true. They talked about her old boyfriends. Some real doozies in that lot. One of those bozos even came forward to have his fifteen minutes of fame.

Silas looked up. "They care about you because of the company you keep." He nodded towards Henryk.

She threw her hands up and I could've told Silas that she didn't want the *honest answer*. She wanted the *feel better answer*. She wanted us to tell her that they would all move on and forget about her.

And when he didn't do that—didn't tell her what she wanted to hear—a new batch of tears slipped down her cheeks. "So, if I want to keep my private life private, I have to give him up? Otherwise, it's open season on me too?"

Henryk had left the room, saying he was going to find this Harlow woman and explain the rules to her. He had to do something because Erin wouldn't survive much more of this.

"Well, Erin, if they're going to write it anyway and talk about you anyway, and photograph you anyway, why let it bother you? Show them you're the kind of badass who doesn't give a shit what they write about you." It was easy for Silas to say.

But I agreed with him. "We're in Spain. And so far, we've gone sightseeing one day and been holed up here the rest of the time." Not that being holed up in a room with her had been all bad. There had been some downright thrilling moments, ones I sure as fuck was not going to forget. But we can't stay in bed all the time.

She picked up the tablet she brought out of the bedroom with her, swiping the screen. "*Party Prince's Panty Wearing Prostitute.*" She slid her finger from left to right. "*Henryk's Honey and Her House of Hunks.*"

Even I could admit it sounded bad, but Silas shrugged. "So, they love alliteration. Who doesn't?"

I almost bit my tongue off. Now was not the time for jokes.

She lifted her head enough to glare at him. "They called me a fucking prostitute, Silas."

"So what? Who cares what they think?" To my way of thinking, this was a whole lot of grumbling over things we couldn't do anything about. The papers weren't going to be *un*published, and the stories were already out there.

"I care. I care so much." She shook her head at me and punched her hands onto her hips. Even angry she was hot enough to make my dick stand up and take notice.

"Why?" I wasn't being a smartass. I really wanted to know why she cared.

"Why?" She turned away from me then spun back. "Why?" Her eyes flashed, darkened. "You may not care what people think about you, but I do. And maybe if this was some local paper, it wouldn't matter. But this fucking thing is national. Everyone from sea to shining sea and pole to fucking pole can see it. And if they don't have newsstands with the hard copy, there's always a fucking blog, right?"

That Harlow person had better hope that Erin didn't get hold of her. It wouldn't be a cat fight or a fist fight, even. It would be an annihilation and when the dust settled, only Erin would be left standing.

But first, we had to get her to calm down and see that it wasn't that big of a deal.

"Look, Erin." Silas held up the iPad she'd just thrown on the sofa. "These are the same pictures as yesterday, just with new headlines. So, they're recycling news."

"Is that supposed to make me feel better?" She smiled but there was no joy in it. It was more a smile of disbelief. "Because it doesn't. Not even a little bit."

"No, I guess not." Silas set the tablet on the table. He'd given it a go and she'd shot him down. There was no point in talking to her if she was just going to continue drowning herself in her misery.

I waited and realized I had to say something. "Look, we're in Ibiza." I specifically called it I-BEEEZ-uh because it always made Fancy Pants roll his eyes and correct me, every time to I-BEETH-uh. But he wasn't here and so there wasn't anyone to tell me different today. "I say that since the articles are already out there and they aren't likely to stop either, we go about our business and see this place. We have the fun we came here to have, and we don't worry about who's doing what, or saying what, or writing what."

"They didn't call you a prostitute." Her words were bitter, but her acidity wasn't pointed at me. It was a response to her situation.

"No, but whatever they say, they're going to say it whether we're holed up here or whether we're out there living our lives and having fun like we planned." It all made sense to me. There was a world outside this hotel I hadn't seen yet, and I could sit and play Call of Duty with Silas at home. It wasn't likely that I was going to get another chance to come to Ibiza or anywhere else. I wasn't broke, dirt poor or impoverished, but travel like this was above my pay grade.

Erin glanced at me, and I could see some of the angry air had come out of her sails.

I shrugged. "I'm just saying that we're here. What's happening to you and Henryk is shit, we all know that, but if we stay in this room, if we don't do the things we planned to do when we left Lichtenstein, then they win. And we can sit inside at home."

Well, figuratively, anyway. Silas and I would technically be outside, back at work. This was a vacation, probably the only one we would get for another year.

She looked at me, then at Silas. "I'm sorry."

I shook my head. "No, Erin, it isn't... you're allowed to feel what you feel, and if you want to stay in the room, that's up to you. But if you do, you're letting them win."

Her expression cleared and she nodded. "And they don't deserve to win."

Now she was coming around and I was relieved. Anger on her was hot, but I much preferred her smile, her happiness. "That's right. What we do is our business."

"Damned right." Silas tossed the game controller onto the table and stood. "When Fancy—erm, Henryk gets back, we can go do something."

She nodded. "Yeah." Her face was still red from crying, and her hair was piled on top of her head in some sort of style that made it look like she had a small bird's nest up there, but it was the smile that made her beautiful.

"So, what should we do today?" Now that we'd decided to do something, I was anxious to get going. I wanted to eat the food, drink the cervezas, enjoy Ibiza the way it was meant to be enjoyed.

"When Henryk gets back with Ray, we can figure it out. Right now, I'm going to get ready." She bounced into the other room, and while she wasn't exactly singing-in-the-shower happy, she'd kicked the music on.

I plopped down by Silas and he nodded at me. "Good talk. I

thought we were going to end up sitting in this hotel room until our flight home."

"I wouldn't mind, considering how everything in the bedroom has been going." Seriously, I could go for a few more rounds of happy time. "But we're here. We're tourists. Might as well do all the things."

It took about twenty-five minutes before Erin came out, refreshed, dressed and ready to move past this. I hoped so, anyway. She was smiling and that, for right now, was enough.

I gave her an appraising look, took in the shine of her hair, the way her smile lit up her entire face. And the body. Fuck. I couldn't stop looking. She had hips that were meant to be held, breasts that were round and perky, with nipples that made little points under her bra and shirt. Her legs were long and tan, and her shorts emphasized the roundness of her ass.

I wanted her. I wanted to feel her soft skin against mine. More, I wanted to kiss her. But it wasn't the time. Instead, I clapped my hands and looked at her.

"What should we do today?" I was open to anything so long as we weren't stuck in the hotel room.

I knew I could go sight-seeing alone or with Silas—no one cared what we did and certainly wouldn't be photographing or documenting it—but I spent every day of my adult life with Silas. I wanted to spend time with Erin. I wanted to see her smile, to watch her tip her head back and close her eyes, absorbing the rays when the sun hit her face. Much as I liked hanging out with Silas, I didn't really come here to vacation with him.

She wobbled her head back and forth as though she were thinking. There were a lot of things to do in Ibiza, but most of them that weren't beach-related happened after dark. The dance clubs, the night life, that was what brought everyone to this part of Spain. "Maybe we should wait for Henryk to get back from his chat with Harlow."

Yeah. We were a team now. It was the four of us against the world.

I wanted her to be happy, wanted to see her smile so I nodded. My stomach clenched suddenly. I didn't have any idea when I'd caught feelings for Erin, but sure enough, they were real and I was scared. The kind of scared that tempted me to run, and hop the next plane home.

I looked at her and Silas, sitting on the sofa now, quiet but waiting for Henryk with their beers and their easy companionship. I couldn't catch a breath, as close to a panic attack as I'd ever been over something I couldn't control. Feelings I didn't want to have. And damned if I knew what to do about it.

CHAPTER 11

Henryk

Harlow was nothing like I imagined. And prior to the moment I stood across from her in the resort's conference room, I wouldn't have ever suspected it was her. A spy. Someone who'd once been invited into the palace to interview my father. I didn't know what sort of fall had sent her crashing to the murky depths of tabloid reporting, but I wanted it to stop.

She was in her forties, probably the latter half, but she had clear skin, wide eyes, and plump lips. She was the kind of woman that even though older was enough to make a man grateful for women.

"Do you have children, Ms. Harlow?" I thought maybe we could establish a rapport.

She nodded and her mouth twisted. "I have two sons." I didn't expect her to haul out the family photos, but she turned her phone toward me. "The brunet is Rhett. He's nineteen, and the older one" – a blond– "is Spencer." She turned the phone back toward herself. "Spencer is married now with a baby on the way." She shoved the phone into her pocket. "I don't suppose you invited me to meet you here" – and by *invited*, she meant I'd sent Raymond to bring her and not given her an opportunity to decline– "to discuss my kids." And she was right, of course.

I nodded. She was a get-down-to-business type of a woman and probably guessed that I was here to make her an offer. There was no real reason not to get to it. "I need the articles to stop."

She nodded and her hair fell over her shoulder. She pushed it back and lifted her gaze to mine. "Of course, you do. But I can't help you, your highness."

"Because it's your job?" It was a good reason, but not good enough. I would match the money and add enough to make it worth her while to stop printing the stories. "What if it isn't your job anymore?"

"Then they'll send someone else." She shrugged like it didn't matter what I did. "You know they will."

"Right. Yes." I paced a few steps away then turned and walked back toward her.

"My editor isn't going to let this go. She smells a story, and she wants it. If you tell me what's going on with you and your... traveling companions, I'll print it, your side, but if you don't tell me, then I won't have a choice but to keep digging until someone gives me the story." I didn't answer one way or the other, but she opened a notebook anyway. "What do you know about the traveling companions you've chosen?"

My blood boiled under my skin. I wanted to scream, to yell at her that this wasn't a story anyone *needed*. Who I slept with was my business and not that of the masses, but she would argue her US Constitution First Amendment rights and the rights of her paper. And then the court battle would be long and tedious, and details would emerge that I didn't want out in the public.

This wasn't up to me, and I wasn't used to things not being up to me. I shot her a glare. "I'm not telling you a fucking thing."

She shrugged and flipped the notebook closed. "Listen, kid." *That wasn't at all insulting.* "I didn't come up with these stories on my own. They're being fed to us." *Of course, they were.*

I rolled my eyes. It was always about money with these types of people. But this one wanted more. Something bigger. "I can offer you a job working in the royal press."

"I have a job." She sighed. "And I have a story about four little seven-year-olds who were on a playground and married each other so they would always have friends." She clicked her tongue against her teeth. Whatever she was going to say wasn't going to be kind or friendly. "A prince, a son of a diplomat, a little girl with blue flower barrettes, and a boy who lived nearby and who turned eight and was sent to juvenile detention until he was fourteen." She shook her head. I didn't know which one of the boys she was talking about, but nothing good would come out of printing the article. "And these are the same people in this hotel right now."

"Who told you about that?" I was pretty desperate for the information. I would pay big for it, too.

"It's a tip we have. The story isn't written yet." She flipped her hair out of her eyes and then pushed the longer strands over her shoulder again.

"But you're going to write it?" I growled the words at her because I couldn't keep the anger out of my tone.

"It's my job."

"It's your *choice.*" I cocked my head, shot her my best king in training glare. "I offered you a job with substance."

"A job in *Lichtenstein*. My family is in Los Angeles." There really wasn't much I could do about the geography. The royal press corps lived where the royal family lived. It was where the stories were.

"We will pay for your move. You'll have your own apartment on the grounds." I promised her a salary that made her eyes go wide and her eyebrows disappear under the hair hanging on her forehead.

"And in exchange, I only have to stop writing articles about you and your friends?" It was a sweet deal to *not* do a job and if she didn't know it or couldn't recognize the opportunity, I couldn't help her. Although I was certainly going to stay here and try. For as long as it took.

"That would definitely contribute to the longevity of your employment." I smiled. "And I would need to know who's feeding you the stories." She had too much information–blue barrettes could've only come from inside the palace where the picture of that day was tucked in a photo album–for it to have been gleaned without a substantial amount of leaking from the palace.

And I couldn't have anyone in the palace who was happy to destroy me.

"I'll need a minute to think about it." But she was considering it. And even if she declined, this consideration might save me one more day from having to explain another article to my mother.

I nodded. "Of course." There wasn't much more I could say to her. And it would be a hard sell to my mother, but I didn't have a choice. My mother, during one of her five calls today, had instructed me to make the stories stop. For the first time in more than eighty years, Lichtenstein was invited to join a summit with the North American and European countries of power where world issues were to be the focus. I was going as ambassador for the king because my father's health was waning.

Every story hurt my credibility and my mother had informed me in one of the calls today that if the stories and the embarrassment continued, my father would send Nicky to the summit in my place.

I still couldn't believe that was the threat. First, Nicky, who'd spent two of his years during secondary school in a drug treatment facility, who'd stolen one of our father's cars and drove it through the north palace wall and then deposited it into the swimming pool. He'd caused more than three million dollars in damage. This was an apples and oranges situation, and I couldn't see Nicky cleaning his act up enough or cutting his hair short enough for my father to consider letting him off the royal palace grounds.

"I'll let you know my decision tomorrow." Tomorrow was soon enough, since I had to tell my mother what I'd promised. She would either be glad I'd found a solution, maybe impressed, or she would be pissed off I'd offered the enemy a job inside the palace.

I left and went back to the suite. Erin and the guys were sitting at the dining table, drinking. I wished I could throw caution to the wind and sit in front of a window with the three of them and drink until the troubles of the world went away. But before I could take a chance like that, I had to figure out how anyone managed to get pictures of us before. I couldn't take a chance that some other tabloid could have caught the scent of this story and descended on the resort.

Just once, I wanted to not have to worry. I wanted to be able to forget who I was and enjoy the same freedom everyone else did. The one time I'd done that, pictures of my dick ended up on nightly world news. But it has been shoddy reporting.

They mingled my history—probably because there wasn't any —with Nicky's. Said after my stint in a California drug treatment facility, I'd flown to Ibiza with my entourage and engaged in illicit group sex, binge drinking, and wild partying at an Ibiza club. It was like they'd read exactly from Harlow's article but added the rehab session to make it more enticing and sensational.

Erin twisted to sit sideways in her chair. "How did it go?"

I shrugged. "I don't know yet. I won't know until tomorrow." I had to wait for Harlow to make a decision,. but I didn't feel as if re-hashing it would serve any purpose.

"Can we go do something now?" Silas stared at me. We'd found a new peace and I didn't want to destroy that with the truth.

So, instead I nodded, and an idea sprouted. If I couldn't be myself and have fun on the grounds at the resort because I couldn't control what was seen and what wasn't, I wouldn't stay on the grounds. There were helicopter tours that would let us see all the things I couldn't risk visiting. For a little while, I could be a part of the group outside of the hotel.

"Yes, let me make the arrangements." I nodded at them because this idea was something that could save this day for all of us.

An hour later we were in the air, wearing the headphones that allowed us to talk to one another over the whir of the propeller. There was nothing like looking down and seeing a pod of dolphins frolicking in the water. Erin clutched my arm and stared with wide eyes.

We flew over the water for a few minutes and Silas grasped his seat hard enough his knuckles were white, a sharp contrast to the green pallor in his cheeks and his skin. "I'll be glad when we're back on the ground," he muttered, but thanks to the microphones attached to the headsets, we all heard him.

After about an hour in the air, we landed and Raymond, waiting with a driver, brought us to a private stretch of beach, miles away from the resort. No one here cared that we hadn't brought suits to swim.

No one cared that one minute Erin kissed Viktor, then in the next, kissed me. No one cared because there was no one around. Private meant deserted. And we played in the water like carefree children.

I'd seen all of Ibiza before, from land, from sea, from air, but I loved hearing Erin and the guys excited over the dolphins, the water, the size of the waves. Fresh eyes made everything feel new.

I hadn't had such a good day in a long time. And when we finally returned to the hotel, I walked into the suite happy. And even if it only lasted for a few minutes, it would be enough to carry me through for a while.

"Hey, Henryk, you've got mail." Silas held up an envelope.

"Put that down!" Oh, God. The lightness of my mood drained instantly and I sounded like an asshole.

It looked like a plain white envelope and my name was written on the front. Handwritten, in ink. There was a group of people at the palace who opened the mail for my mother and father, sometimes for me. They wore special clothing–gloves, masks—and left no skin exposed in case someone sent mail with some sort of drug or chemical toxin on the envelope. "Put that down!" I said it again because it was important.

Silas dropped the envelope. "God. It's just an envelope Henryk."

I gave him the explanation and he shrugged.

"You have to lighten up, your highness." He wasn't taking it seriously, but not everyone believed my family should rule. Not everyone was a fan or royal watcher and considering that I was doing what some considered purposely disgracing my crown, I couldn't take a chance.

Raymond wrapped one of the cloth napkins from the dining table around his hand and took the envelope and held it up to the light. I couldn't see anything but paper.

Then Ray carefully opened the envelope and investigated it.

"All right. Here." He held it so I could read it, but he still wouldn't let me touch it. When I tried, he pulled it back and shook his head. "Henryk."

I sighed. The letter was from Harlow. She wanted me to meet her. I nodded at Raymond, and he walked a few steps toward the kitchenette, dropped the letter into the garbage bin and pulled out his phone. He made a quiet call then nodded at me.

"What is it?" Erin laid her hand on my shoulder.

"Harlow wants to talk." I shrugged. "And I need to know if she's going to write the story she told me about."

"What story?"

I shrugged. "Just more of the same. Someone tipped her off about the wedding when we were kids. The spin won't be good or innocent. It'll make a game we played innocently seem tawdry, planned." That was the last thing I wanted, but if I couldn't work out a deal with Harlow, it would happen and I needed Erin to know, to prepare herself.

She nodded and pulled me down for a kiss. "Good luck, Henryk. And if it doesn't work, we'll figure it out." When we broke apart, she stepped back and nodded. "Don't worry. We're here for you."

She looked back over her shoulder at Silas and Viktor, who were turned from their video game to watch us.

"You bet, man. We've got your back." Viktor nodded at me, and Silas stuck a thumb up into the air, his arm behind him as he used the game controller with his other hand to command the screen and start a game.

Again, I wished for that kind of easiness in life. Nicky had found it a long time ago. Now I wanted it. But first, I had to deal with Harlow, and then my mother.

When I arrived, Harlow was already waiting in the same conference room where we'd met before.

"Ms. Harlow." I nodded at her, and she lifted her head as if she wasn't expecting to hear my voice.

But then she smiled. "Your highness." She shook her head. "I wasn't sure if you were going to come."

I smiled at her. "I have a vested interest in your answer."

She stared at me for a full three seconds before she nodded. I stood with my arms crossed and waited. She knew why I was here. I only wanted an answer.

"I have a counter-proposal for you."

I nodded. "All right. What do you want?"

Whatever it was, it was big enough she didn't look at me while she gathered her courage to ask for it. It took a few seconds before she lifted her gaze. "I want the job as the royal recorder."

The royal recorder was a person on the staff at the palace who lived at the palace, traveled with the king or queen, sometimes with the ambassador, and documented all royal business. It was a position that required trust from the crown and no way in hell would my mother let a tabloid reporter have the job.

"And if I give you that job, you will stop writing articles and you'll tell me who's providing the information?" I needed her word. Maybe even her to put it in writing.

"I'll tell you what I know." She nodded. "But I don't know who's sending the information."

Of course, she didn't. No one at the palace would be stupid enough–and I was still convinced it had to be someone on the inside–to leave a name, a calling card, something that revealed an identity. But maybe having my own covert operative on the inside wouldn't be a wholly bad idea.

We shook hands and I smiled. "Miss Harlow, we have a deal."

She grinned with more enthusiasm than I'd seen so far. "I'll go home and start packing. But be careful. I'm not the only reporter who's here. Be discreet." She gave me a wink. "And I'll see you in Lichtenstein."

"I'll have my valet make the arrangements."

Raymond would hate that I'd demoted him from personal security to personal shopper, but he was a multi-purpose employee. For today he would deal with it. And tomorrow, I would deal with everything else.

CHAPTER 12

Erin

When Henryk returned to the suite, he was in a much better mood. I'd heard him whistling before he even opened the door. And then he came in and Fred Astaire'd me around the living room part of the suite, humming some tune that was horribly off-key, but I couldn't help but smile. Laugh. Then he dipped me back and kissed me as he brought me upright again.

"You're beautiful, Erin." He grinned and lifted me off my feet. This was the Henryk I knew was in there. Fun and carefree. "Let's go to the beach!" He clapped his hands together then joined in the whooping when Silas and Viktor started the chorus of it.

I watched them and my heart was full. Joyous. Happy. I cared about them all so much. Silas laughed, high-fiving Viktor. They both grabbed Henryk in some weird frat-boy kind of bear hug. I laughed along because what else could I do? It was incredible to see them all getting along.

When I went into the bedroom to get ready, they were all still in the main room of the suite. But it was as I was changing that Henryk opened the door and walked in. I was facing away and turned to look at him over my shoulder. "Hi."

He closed the door and smiled as he leaned back against it. He didn't move or speak.

"You all right?" I called out, unsure of what his next move was going to be.

His gaze was intense, like a physical touch against my cheek. He pushed off the door and prowled toward me. I had just tied my bikini top around my neck, and he slipped his hands under my ponytail and untied the little bow I'd put there, then turned me to face him.

"Henryk?" I asked, breathless now.

He kissed my throat then my shoulder, and then the curve of my breast. My back arched toward him, wanting more. He pulled the top of the bikini down so he could cup my breast with his hand and swirl my aching nipple with his tongue. I curled my fingers into his hair and held on while he licked and sucked at me.

I loved watching him there, the visual stimulation doubling the physical pleasure pulsing through me.

He stepped back for a second then smiled as he moved to kneel in front of me. As he went down, he dragged my swimsuit bottoms with him, then stared up at me.

I couldn't stop myself from reaching out and cupping his face with my palm. I had a prince on his knees in front of me, and my heart couldn't be any fuller.

He slid the backs of his hands up the inside of my thighs, and I gasped at the new sensations each touch caused.

When his tongue swiped my clit, my knees shook. I half sighed, half moaned. "Henryk..." His name was a whisper because

I couldn't manage more. He lifted my leg and laid it over his shoulder and slid a finger inside me, pulled it out and pushed a second finger in. Oh, God, he was incredible.

This was amazing. My body tightened too quickly. I wanted to savor this moment, wanted to draw out the pleasure, but I couldn't. I was too close to toppling over the edge.

My orgasm exploded inside me, and I cried out, grasped a handful of his hair and held him to me. *Oh, God.* I rode the waves of passion until I slowly spiraled back down, and my legs could once again hold me without his help.

I extricated myself and smiled. "That was incredible." And it was.

He stood up and kissed my cheek. "I'll shower and be out in a few minutes."

We still had plenty of daylight left and enough time to have fun together, but I wasn't certain I wanted to go out. Having my name and my personal business put out there for the world to read was traumatizing, especially since it was given such a negative spin. They'd called me a prostitute.

Everyone I knew would've read that article. Not that we were gossip mongers, but seeing my picture on the front of a gossip rag would garner their interest. Bree had certainly taken note of it.

My parents too... probably. I'd need to call them when I could. Though what I was going to say, I had no idea.

I pulled my bikini back on and put on a short skirt that tied at the hip. The skirt was the same turquoise as my suit and was feminine and pretty.

I walked out of the room while Henryk was still showering. My nerves were shaken at the thought of going to a beach now that people knew who we were. Or who they thought I was, anyway.

I'd never been unsettled like this before, so shaky. It wasn't normal for me. I didn't suffer the symptoms of insecurity. Not that I was arrogant, I just didn't generally have an issue with self-consciousness or nerves. But today, I wanted to cover up, maybe not go to the beach at all.

Why oh why did I bring all bikinis?

However, when I walked out into the suite's common area, Silas and Viktor were already in their swimming trunks.

Silas smiled at me. "Damn, girl. You are wearing that bikini." His gazed raked over me, heating my skin everywhere it touched. And he was thorough.

It was only a few minutes after that Henryk walked out and we left for the beach. The car— an SUV with blacked-out windows— sped us along the coast to a part of the beach that belonged to the resort and was used for VIP guests who had privacy concerns. I didn't know how Henryk, or more likely Ray, had managed to secure its use by us, but it helped ease my anxiety fractionally.

Ray and Henryk were in the front seat, and I sat in the back between Silas and Viktor, but the conversations went on around me without any input on my part. And now, along with my moderate social discomfort, my stomach was a tight, painful ball.

Ray pulled the vehicle into the cove lot. He parked and the guys all climbed out. I sat for a moment, wondering how big a deal it would be if I just stayed in the car and read a book. Probably would've been more convincing if I'd brought a book along.

I slid out and walked around the back to where Silas was pulling out one of the resort's coolers he'd had stocked with beer.

There was also a picnic basket of fruit, cheese, nuts and some water bottles. Ray retrieved a fold-up umbrella and Henryk pulled some folding chairs from the back. Someone had packed a very detail-oriented trunk, and I smiled.

There was no one else in this cove and while I could see the back side of the resort from here, I was confident they couldn't see us. It made stepping out of the skirt and playing in the water not as daunting as the idea had been when we were on our way here.

The water rolled in on the beach and we played for a few minutes, but I couldn't relax, couldn't stop feeling as though we were being watched. I stopped every few minutes and stared, looked around, checked the cliffs that made this into a cove, but I couldn't see much of anything.

There were a couple of birds hovering, gulls, as far as I could tell, but then a larger black bird flew in closer. I gasped when I focused on the shape. It wasn't a bird at all but a drone, a four-propeller, smooth, plastic drone with some sort of insignia painted on the bottom.

Silas was out surfing. Viktor was swimming in the deeper water and Henryk was tossing an American football back and forth on the beach with Ray. I stood, using the umbrella to try to bat the drone out of the sky. It was being "driven" from a remote location, but it obviously had a camera eye and could see what I was doing. It responded to my rabid swinging of the umbrella by climbing higher and higher and then flying up the cliff and out of sight.

That's when I saw the crest on the bottom of the damned thing.

Fucking bastards.

Henryk and Ray were already near and coming toward me.

The umbrella was heavy now, much more so than when I was swinging it at the offending drone. I dropped it near the picnic basket. It thudded onto the sand and that quickly, they were all there.

"Are you all right?" Henryk laid his hands on my shoulder.

I nodded even though my heart was beating hard enough it could have easily pounded through my sternum. "Yeah." And then I looked at Henryk. "It was a drone."

"A drone?" He cocked his head as if he thought maybe he hadn't heard me clearly. "Are you sure?"

Of course, I was sure. "Yeah. I'm positive." I sure as hell wouldn't have acted that way over a bird. And he needed to know the rest. "It had the royal crest on it."

It made sense. This pointed to someone in his world following us. And it could've been to see what he was up to, could've been to watch him to prevent him from more of what they thought was illicit behavior. Although I couldn't work my head around seeing how that made sense. How would they stop him by watching? And certainly not by watching me.

"Royal crest?" His eyes narrowed but he lowered his voice like he didn't want the others to hear what I was saying.

"Yeah. The one painted on the ceiling in your castle and inlaid in the floor." The Lichtenstein royalty certainly liked showing off their crest. "Otherwise, I wouldn't have recognized it."

I looked at Henryk, but he looked at Ray, and like they communicated telepathically, Ray pulled a phone from his pocket, turned away and dialed as he walked down the beach.

I stared at Henryk. "I want to go back to the resort." I wanted to go home. To my home in the States. But that wasn't likely to happen just yet. We had two days left before our flight.

"All right." They all started gathering our things, and I helped despite Henryk's protests because I was the one making everyone leave, and I needed to do something. Anything other than sitting and worrying while they did all the packing.

I continued checking the sky. I hadn't managed to even touch the damned drone with the umbrella, and I figured whoever was operating it hadn't seen anything untoward or tabloid worthy, so it would be back. I was sure of that.

CHAPTER 13
Silas

The ride back to the hotel was subdued. And by subdued, it could've been described as deathly silent. Angry silent. Wholly silent. Ray hadn't even turned the radio on. The only real sound was the occasional burst of Erin's breath as a sigh or a gush. I took her hand and held it because I thought she needed the contact. But when she pulled away, shook her head and pulled her shoulders into her body as small as possible as if she was trying to be invisible, I didn't push. This was bothering her in ways I hadn't realized.

The prince might've been used to having his life broadcast as entertainment for the masses and that was fine. For him. But for Erin, she was devastated. It wasn't in anything she said or anything she did. It was an expression, a feeling, and it consumed her.

"Hey." She turned her head toward me, but I got the feeling she wasn't looking at me. She wasn't seeing me. There was a glaze over her expression, as if she was trying to shield herself by not focusing. "Erin?"

She didn't speak, she shook her head instead. Looked past me out the window. This was a lot for her to deal with, and if she needed a minute to pull her head together, I could give her that, but I wasn't going to let it go on for much past a minute. I wasn't going to let her fall into this rhythm of sadness.

I'd known someone who drowned in her sadness before–a beautiful girl named Nicole who'd been a college friend. She'd never been able to pull herself out of it.

I wasn't going to let that happen to Erin. I couldn't. I'd already fallen for her. Maybe I'd fallen for her fifteen years ago when she married all of us. Or maybe it was the first time I saw her at the palace, and she'd smiled me and hugged me like it hadn't been more than a decade since we'd seen one another.

It didn't matter when the falling had happened. Only that it *had* happened. And I was sure of it now, and it didn't matter if she wasn't as into me as I was into her. It didn't matter if she wanted all of us instead of one exclusively. It only mattered that I had real, honest, strong feelings for her.

The realization was staggering. Not because I was afraid of it. I wasn't. But because I'd never felt so... whole. She gave that to me. And I wanted to hang onto it, hold it, make it last forever, if I could.

I stared at her. She had a glowing tan, a smile that could break a heart, or stop it, or make it pound. And she was beautiful, even in this sadness that right now seemed to be emanating from her.

When she looked at me, I smiled and would've leaned in and kissed her, but she laid her head on my shoulder and her hand on my thigh. Not high up. Not sexual at all. The move was about comfort.

I breathed in the scent of her shampoo, which like nothing I'd ever smelled before. I could've happily inhaled her all day long, with her head on my shoulder and her hand in my lap.

But the car rolled to a stop, and she lifted her head, pulled her hand away, sat straight again and the tension was thick on her once more, like armor.

She sat in the car for a couple of seconds after the rest of us climbed out and then when she slid to the door and put one foot out, she looked up first, as though she expected the drone to be hovering over the car, waiting for her.

But it wasn't. There was nothing to be seen.

She didn't run inside. Didn't even hurry. But she continued looking up, left and right, waiting for whatever it was she was afraid of to happen. And it affected every part of her from her walk to her stance, to the way she averted her eyes.

I couldn't stand to see her so distressed. She was a magical woman, and someone had taken that light from her. I wanted that person's head on a plate.

Viktor was big and brawny, the kind of guy people were scared of. I was scrappy, the surprise in a fight because I might not have looked it, but I was strong and fast. And I struck without fear. For her, I would take on the world. And it looked like I might have to.

We walked inside together, surrounding her so that she wouldn't be alone in this, although I couldn't be certain she realized it. This had her on a ledge and if we didn't figure out fast how to talk her down, there was likely to be something tragic that resulted.

When the door to the suite closed behind us, she sat heavily on the sofa and tilted her head up to the ceiling, eyes closed. "I'm sorry I'm such a downer." Her voice was soft but there was honest pain in her tone. It made it weaker, deadening the usual vibrance.

Henryk sat beside her on one side, and I sat on the other. And this time, instead of leaning on the prince, instead of being "with" him, she put her head on my shoulder, shifted away from him and closer to me. She was blaming him, and it was easy to see.

As much as I enjoyed her beside me, her hand on my chest, her body nestled into mine, it wasn't fair to blame Henryk for this.

"Erin?" She lifted her head and looked at me. "I know this sucks, but it isn't Henryk's fault."

She scoffed and now, she shifted away from me. "I know that."

"The drone she saw was painted with the royal crest." He looked down at his hands as he slowly rubbed his palms together. When he stood and walked to the outer door to the patio, Erin didn't follow.

"Erin?" She looked at me. "I know this sucks. If I could get my hands on that Harlow person or the editor or the guy who owns that fucking paper, I would tear them apart for you." She half-smiled and nodded. "But this isn't really Henryk's fault."

She nodded. "I know."

"Princes are forgiven for what the public thinks are missteps as soon as they're kings." I certainly didn't want to imply that this was a misstep, only that others might perceive it as such. This wasn't a kind of life that all people could understand, or that they would want for themselves. I, personally, didn't understand the need to judge others, but I wasn't the norm. I was more the exception. People judged. It wasn't unusual.

"I know. But I have to get my head around it all."

I nodded. If it were me, I would probably do the things I said I would do for her. I would find Harlow and her editor and the guy who owned the paper. And things would unfurl as they happened. But I couldn't do that now or I would lose Erin.

From where I sat, I could see Henryk outside on the patio, speaking on the phone and gesturing. He was the kind of guy who spoke with his hands when he was flustered and apparently, he was more and more flustered by the minute.

I stood up. "I'll be right back." It was worth it to me to find out who he was talking to. This was bad for both of them, which made it bad for all of us. But I wanted him to know he wasn't without friends too. We were in this together.

When I walked outside, Henryk was speaking in a low, controlled tone. "Goddammit! I know it's you." And then he was quiet for a moment. "What the fuck purpose does this serve you, you little shit?" Another pause. "Oh, you think so? Where are you? I'll find you right now and beat your ass all the way home." Another pause and I could feel the prince's rage vibrating off him. "You'll never be king, Nicky. You don't have the strength for it and no one in any country will follow an eighteen-year-old drug addict." He hit end, and then threw his phone so hard it bounced over the fence and onto the beach.

"Nicky?" I cocked an eyebrow at him, and when he turned to see me he startled.

"Maybe you should wear a bell." He shook his head and punched his hands onto his hips. "Eavesdropping?"

"Not really. Just came out to make sure you're handling this okay." He was angry, would've probably been happy to take it out on me.

He shook his head. "Do I look okay?" And then he chuckled. "Some vacation, right?"

I shrugged. It hadn't been wholly bad. "It happens." But I was curious as to who Nicky was and why he thought he... or she could have been the one watching us with the drone.

His sigh came from somewhere deeper than a lung. It took all the height from his shoulders, so they slumped. "My brother, Nickolai. Turns out, the little shit wants the crown. Playing dirty to get it."

"Oh." Now that was a family issue I didn't feel like I was in a position to comment on.

"And he's here somewhere, likely at this fucking resort." It was probably a good thing his brother wasn't here, or Henryk might have gone medieval on him.

And by the time it was finished, there wouldn't be a contest for the throne. Only one of them would remain standing. I had never seen the brother, but my money was on Henryk.

Henryk had the determination and if his viciousness was anything like what he displayed when we played video games–Call of Duty brought out his inner savage–the brother didn't stand a chance.

"Why does anyone care what you do? What does it matter?" I just didn't understand it. "As long as you're doing your job, what difference does it make?"

"It's about trust." He sighed again, raked his fingers through his hair, and turned.

But none of it made his answer any clearer for me. And, of course, that didn't matter, either. What mattered was that for this to be successful with us and Erin, we had to do our parts, make it work, decide that no part was greater than the sum of what we had as a group.

I could keep his secrets, and I would. For Erin. For all of us. So long as the fun didn't come to a crashing halt, and no one–Fancy Pants or not–got too big for their britches. If that happened, all bets were off.

CHAPTER 14
Viktor

The thing about me was that while everyone else was happy to sit around talking about their *feelings* and how to solve a problem without actually doing anything to solve it, I was the guy who went in guns blazing, solving problems in a way that begged no question that the problem was, indeed, solved.

This wasn't going to be different, and I didn't need anyone's permission to act. Not Silas' for sure. And I wondered about him because once upon a time, he'd been as much like me as a guy could get without being me. He wouldn't have stuck around asking if everyone was okay. He would've gone out, found the person who wrote the article, and that person wouldn't have been a problem anymore.

Now he was sitting on the sofa beside Erin and the prince, and he was consoling them while I drank. This was more than a beer kind of situation. This one called for whiskey. And I drank

And drank.

Shot after shot.

Until finally, all the whining was too much. "What the fuck?" I didn't shout the words, but they all turned toward me and stared like I was pounding my chest, some kind of Incredible Hulk spectacle. "What?" I stared at Silas. "You got something to say?"

He shook his head. "Maybe take a breath between drinks, pal."

I threw my hands up. "Look, I'm not going to let some little jerk with a drone ruin our time in Spain." I walked around the corner bar where the alcohol was stored. Silas knew everything about me, but the others didn't. And it was time to share.

I picked up Fancy Pants' laptop and popped open the lid. I didn't even need the password, I was that good.

"What are you doing?"

"Well, before I decided that I liked building things, I decided I was going to learn how to do whatever I wanted on a computer." I typed code while I spoke. Could do this in my sleep. "Right now, I'm looking for any invader to the Wi-Fi." There wasn't anyone stealing it. "And now I'm looking for someone who was using it twenty-five minutes ago here and remotely. The drone sends out a remote signal." Any explanation more complicated and I would lose the impact of what I was saying.

Henryk stood behind me now watching over my shoulder. "If you can do all this...you could make so much money..."

Yeah. I got that question a lot back in the day. "It isn't like I'm living on the streets. Back then, though, the cops kept shutting me down. Threatening me with jail." I shrugged. Those had been the good old days. I remembered them fondly. I back traced the IP address then tapped the webcam of the person receiving the feed from the camera on the drone.

I'd forgotten how much fun this was.

I took a screen shot, expanded the photo and turned the computer so Silas and Erin could also see.

It was a kid. Blond and the family resemblance was unmistakable. I turned to look at the prince.

Henryk shook his head but remained silent. Instead of looking at the picture, he looked down at his hands.

But it was Erin who scoffed then said, "You knew?"

"I suspected. Hell, I even accused. That's who I was talking to outside." He shook his head. "That is my younger brother, Nickolai. I was the heir, he was the spare." This time, he was a bit more flippant, and his eyes narrowed. "I can't believe he's doing this."

But we had proof. I could prove it all day long. "I could shoot a virus through to his computer." That wasn't rocket science. A couple lines of code and he'd be at my mercy. "I can disable it completely or just send him a little something so every time he logs on, it will shuffle to porn. Hell, I can monitor every single thing he does, if you want. Have his keystrokes shoot to the same tabloids he's feeding his stories to." I shrugged. It was up to Henryk.

"Good to know. Don't piss off Viktor." Silas laughed. Obviously, he knew I had this skill. He'd known me since I could remember, but he was doing everything he could to try to lighten the heaviness in the room.

"We all already know you watch porn," I said and laughed.

He nodded and smiled. "It passes the time." If someone didn't stop him, we were going to have to hear about–and possibly watch–his favorite scenes, favorite actresses, favorite everything about his personal choices for nightly viewing. "I mean, nobody watches them for more than a couple minutes, but..." He shrugged again.

I cleared my throat. "Is your brother here in Ibiza?" I-BEEZ-uh.

Henryk shook his head. "Nicky must have one of his staff here operating the drone. If he was here, there would've been a story. Someone would've photographed it, and the headline would've been something about Lichtenstein princes vacay together or something equally dumb."

"Maybe not, since they have so much other stuff to write about." The prince's sex life probably trumped his brother's vacation plans. But I didn't say more. There wasn't a point, since the subject seemed to be so touchy for them.

Erin stood and walked, pacing back and forth on the side of the room away from the windows and doors. I loved watching her. She had a certain kind of grace when she moved, like every step blended into the next. And she was lithe, beautiful and moved like a gazelle.

She paced a few more laps then sighed. "Do we know for certain that it's him? That it's Henryk's brother?" She spoke with a slight venom to her tone. A feistiness that made her more than fierce.

I didn't know what difference it made, or what she planned to do about it, but I nodded. "We know it's him." I had the picture.

"That little shit. What did we ever do to him?" The anger was inching ever closer to rage.

"He wants to be king." Henryk said.

Her eyes flashed and Henryk stood, went to her, ran his hands down her arms to her wrist. "He sees you as collateral damage."

She shook her head and smiled, not one of her wide, beautiful smiles, but one that was about half strength. Not that it wasn't beautiful, but it wasn't *the* one we were all used to. "If I run into that little snot rag, I'll show him damage."

Henryk nodded. "I should've known this had his fingerprints all over it." He shook his head. "He thinks being king will get him laid more. All it's going to get him is Posy. It's written."

It's written. That sounded ominous. Honestly, poor little rich boys had family problems like the rest of us. His were just on a different kind of scale.

Although, the younger prince probably had plans beyond those of marrying some princess from another country. To my way of thinking, Henryk had spent a long time being the good boy and wasted years of using his status as a crown prince in just the way little bro wanted to.

"Your brother's what? Eighteen? Nineteen? And he has staff?" Silas looked at Henryk, who glanced away from Erin long enough to smile.

"We've had our own staff since we were each two years old." Henryk said it like it was a normal thing for a two-year-old to have "staff."

Erin shook her hands free of his and crossed her arms. "I don't care if that spoiled little shit has someone who's going to take his beating for him. One is coming."

This was a feistier Erin than I'd ever seen before. And it was hot.

"I'm so tired of this. I just want it all to stop."

I had to agree. If that little shit ruined this for us, I would happily punish him myself.

CHAPTER 15

Erin

I hated that I ruined the day for all of them. First, I couldn't enjoy even five seconds of the beach and seeing that drone certainly didn't help. I probably should've apologized again. Probably should've been more concerned with the moment I was in, rather than the ones that were being spoken about in the media. I wouldn't have changed my life for anyone else's, or the things I wanted, or the men I was with. I wasn't ashamed.

I wasn't even ashamed of my past. I just didn't expect it to be written about for the entire world to read.

To be fair, I didn't think anyone could've expected such a thing. But in my case, I thought people were better than that. I didn't realize how much it would hurt, either, when the people of my past betrayed me. I was so naive, I had no idea that there were people who would print lies. And they were lying about my past. About me being a prostitute. I stupidly thought that the media couldn't lie.

I wasn't a huge fan of live and learn lessons. But there were mistakes I wouldn't make again, and giving trust was one of them. I sat on the sofa between Silas and Viktor as they played Call of Duty. They were shouting orders at each other, shooting, standing and plopping back down. It was an action-packed game. Like a Stallone or Schwarzenegger movie, but with less plot and more mayhem, although not by much.

It was entertaining, at least. And after a few minutes I had to leave because watching the snipers or whatever was giving me chest pains.

Henryk was reading a stack of paperwork that he'd had Raymond retrieve for him, though I had no idea where they'd originated.

So I went into the bedroom. I wanted to call Bree. Maybe I just needed to hear her voice, to ground myself where I was confident and strong. Right now, I needed some of that.

I dialed her number and waited. I wasn't sure of the time difference, but she would answer. I thought it was only eight or nine hours, but I couldn't be sure.

She answered on the second ring. "Erin! How are you?"

I wanted to give her an honest answer but I'd spent all day making these guys miserable based on my mood. I didn't want to do it to Bree too. "Ibiza is so pretty. And we're all getting along really well."

"Oh, I'm so happy for you."

And I didn't doubt her. She was the most genuine person I'd ever known.

And she wouldn't lie to me. "Have any more stories come out?"

She sucked in a breath. "The first round wasn't bad enough for you?"

"Oh, yeah. It was real joyride." My tone was dry, but she would ignore the sarcasm. I ignored hers enough.

"I haven't seen anything new." She sighed. "How is everything there?"

"Tense." There was nothing sarcastic in this answer. "It's been a rough day. The magazine article was bad enough, but now there's some sort of Lichtenstein drone watching us." I told her about the beach. "I tried to whack it with one of the hotel's umbrellas, but the damned thing was too heavy."

"Oh, God. You should've gone full Barry Bonds on its ass and smacked that bad boy straight over the fence." There was no fence, but I didn't bother to correct her. "Why would Lichtenstein send a drone?" Now wasn't that the just million-dollar question. "Is it military? It would have to be for it to be controlled from that far away."

I was sure Viktor would have mentioned it. "I think the guys said someone is here controlling it but feeding it back to Lichtenstein." I hadn't paid a whole lot of attention to that part since I didn't care about the logistics. I wanted to know who was doing it and if we could make it stop.

"Hmph. Isn't technology something? I mean really." She sounded honestly amazed. I would've been, too, if this was happening to anyone but me. On a day where I hadn't been made the feature of a tawdry story, I enjoyed technology. Used it. Loved it.

This day, though, I wished the world was back to landlines and letter writing. And movies were at the theater. I couldn't really remember a time without cell phones, but I saw Pretty in Pink. Life back then was simpler. Easier. And less stressful.

Right now, I had reached my stress quota for a day, so the

thought of never seeing my name in print, hearing a phone ring while I was at the beach, watching a movie with nothing to worry about but the plot and the popcorn sounded divine in a way nothing else did. Thanks to technology, I'd had quite enough.

"How are things at home?" I would have loved to hear something normal. A date where the guy had fallen madly in love with her. Bree wasn't the love them and leave them type, she was love and be loved until morning light. Then she left. Sometimes she called back or took the call back that always came, but she never got attached. It just wasn't who she was.

"I went on a date the other night–two nights ago–with a guy who works at some fancy law firm, and let me tell you, I almost fell asleep in my Arugula salad." She laughed. "I don't know if it's possible for a man to be more boring than he was." She laughed, but I had a thought. Maybe boring was the way to go. Maybe this–my three husbands–was too much for me to handle and deal and process. Maybe I wasn't strong enough.

But what would I do without them? Not just the sex, but the support and the laughter, the happiness that they brought me was all irreplaceable. I had a pretty great situation going on and so what if the world thought it was a little unorthodox? It certainly was. And so what if the world thought I was a prostitute? I wasn't. I knew it. Silas, Viktor, and Henryk knew it. No one else really mattered.

I stared at the ceiling because at some point, I'd reclined onto the bed. As she finished telling me about her date, I pictured how animated she'd always been when she talked. She was a hand talker, a gesticulator, which sounded dirty when one of her dates had said it and she'd laughed, but then looked it up and admired that he'd used the word.

As she told me about a new boutique that opened on the square–a city block with stores, shoppes and businesses on the interior and exterior of the block– back home, my phone beeped with another call waiting to be answered. I looked at the screen. It was my boss. I'd promised him an answer then missed my own deadline.

"Hey, Bree, I have to go. Bossy Bosserson is on the line, and I have to talk to him." Although I had no idea what I wanted to say. The job was an opportunity. A good one. But so were Silas, Viktor, and Henryk.

"Call me later." And she hung up so that now my phone trilled its shrill ring aloud.

I took a breath and slid my finger over the screen to answer. There was a ball of nerves in the pit of my stomach, and I laid my hand over the spot, hopeful the rolling and bouncing around the ball was doing would stop.

It was a cell. Of course, I knew who was calling and could've greeted him as such, but my brain and mouth had achieved full disconnect, so I went traditional instead of familiar. Could've called him Joffrey, or Joff, or even said, *Hello, Mr. Vandeloo,* but I went with the ever eloquent, "Hello."

"Erin, I'm glad I caught you." Again, I didn't know the time difference. I only knew we were mid-afternoon. They had to be early morning? Or was it early evening? Time confused me.

"Mr. Vandeloo..." I had no idea what I was about to say.

"Erin, the client has decided to go a different way with the account." He blurted the words then paused, presumably so I could burst into tears.

I didn't, but it was early still in the call. "Another way?"

He sighed. "In light of your recent... publicity, they would prefer to work with Jane Rogan."

Jane Rogan? We'd come into the company at the same time. She wasn't nearly as smart or as intuitive as me. She couldn't read a room and wouldn't have known a good idea if she shook hands with it. "My recent publicity?"

And, of course, it was that.

"They just wanted someone a bit less controversial on the team." There was a certain bitterness to his tone. "So, they chose Jane."

It was my turn to sigh. He could say whatever he wanted, but the client wouldn't have known that Jane was available unless Joffrey himself told them. "All right."

"Look, Erin. You still have a job. And I still want you on Jane's team, so I'll still need you back by Monday."

On Jane's team. That made Jane my boss. Swallowing pride was never one of my greater talents, but as I hadn't made a decision yet about what I planned to do with my life, I murmured a "Mm-hmm."

"This isn't a demotion, Erin. You'll still have a great amount of creative input. You just won't be the one pitching the ideas to the client." He made it sound as if I would be integral, but we both knew that with Jane at the helm of the account, I would be fetching coffee and hunting down print ads from the graphics department. I would be a gopher. Might as well call it what it was– a nothing. And I would sell my soul to Satan himself before I gave her a single idea to use or pitch. If the client wanted Jane, they could have her. All of her.

But I needed the job. I couldn't go back home, keep my apartment or eat, without a job. "Okay."

"It's just until this all blows over, Erin."

Sure, it is.

"I'll see you on Monday."

I didn't correct him because I didn't know yet what my plan was going to be. But we hung up and more than ever, I wanted to go kick Nickolai in his baby maker.

I tossed my phone onto the bed beside me and stood up. I couldn't just sit in this room all day and mope. There were things to be done. A vacation to have. Decisions could wait. For a minute, anyway.

When I walked out into the living area of the suite, Silas and Viktor were watching some sort of game on television. I didn't stare hard at it because I didn't care. The announcers were speaking Spanish and I didn't speak enough of it to be able to follow along. Henryk was seated at the table reading a bundle of paperwork and I needed a drink.

The fridge behind the bar was stocked with spritzers and beer, white wine and some hard liquor. I pulled out some Caribbean rum, poured it into a glass and added juice. I wasn't really a bartender, so my concoction might've clashed, but it didn't matter because I drank it in one long gulp.

Henryk, who'd looked up from his paperwork to watch me, smiled. "Are you okay?"

That was a million-dollar question. I hadn't the foggiest idea. But then Silas and Viktor looked up. Silas came to the bar, Viktor remained on the sofa but turned his body to look at me.

"What's wrong?"

I poured myself another drink and added ice cubes this time. I wasn't going to suck this one down in one go. This one was bigger. A sipper.

I glanced at Silas. "I was passed over for a promotion and if I want to keep my crappy job, I have to be back at work on Monday."

Silas smiled sadly. "Real life has come calling."

It certainly had and I wasn't interested. My real life had taken a turn because my fantasy life had spilled over onto it. Henryk watched me and his gaze burned, maybe because I could see the sadness in it. Maybe because I wanted him to ask me to stay with him and he was silent, motionless.

Hell, for all I knew, he could've been in an open-eyed coma.

"Yeah, and it's not been kind." I don't add that it was because of Henryk's brother.

He knew. Everyone here knew.

"What do you want to do?"

"I have to go home. I have an apartment there. All my stuff." But I would miss them. So much. The laughs. The easy conversations, the smiles. And the sex. Oh, God, the sex. "I have rent and bills to pay." I didn't even know what was left anymore.

"That's okay." Silas laid his hand on mine. "There are planes and trains, automobiles. This doesn't have to be the end."

But I glanced at Henryk. It did, and we all knew it. There was no way for us to maintain this kind relationship when we were scattered across the globe.

I sighed. "I think we all know what's going to happen when we get back." And in case they were unclear... "Henryk is going to have to marry his princess. I'm going to have to go back to my job. And you guys have a business to run. None of us can just up and leave anything."

Silas shook his head. "We're all here. And that's something."

Yes, it was something that was about to come to an end. And

as sad as that made me, I wasn't going to let it ruin the time we had left. I just needed a few more minutes to wallow in my sadness–I hoped it was only a few minutes, anyway–and then I would be back to my normal self. And if I couldn't do it alone, there were plenty of little bottles of rum to help me get there.

CHAPTER 16

Henryk

When I became king, I fully intended to lock my brother, that ungrateful turd of a human being, in a dungeon in some rancid castle the family had long ago neglected. And if I failed to find one dank and dark enough in Lichtenstein, I was going to call a cousin in England and see if I could borrow one of theirs. They had castles to spare and underground cellars no one talked about anymore that my cousin, the king, would happily lend to me.

This was an old family threat that my father had used on an uncle of mine. Uncle Vladimir. He was a second son, also. And maybe the one whispering the poison in Nicky's ears. Who knew. All I could say for certain was that Uncle Vlad–a man who closely enough resembled my father for a second I wondered how much younger than my father he was–no longer associated with the royal family. Not with more than a constant threat of overthrow reported occasionally in the papers, so I'd only met him once, but

I had a feeling he was more like Nicky than my father had ever admitted.

I glanced at Erin and my anger at my brother increased yet again. She was taking this all so badly, and I couldn't blame her. She hadn't grown up on the wrong side of the tabloids. She hadn't been forced to deal with this kind of blatant lying in her life, so her behavior was understandable.

But I went to her anyway. Put my arms around her, held her. And when I rubbed her back and she turned her chin up, closed her eyes and pulled me down, I kissed her. Because not kissing her would've been insanity on a level even I couldn't reach.

Of all the things I loved doing with her, kissing her was in the top three. And so, I would do it at every opportunity that presented itself. This was an opportunity.

She curled her fingers into my hair and tugged, not hard, just enough to let me know she wanted something more. I lifted her onto the bar top, and she made the kiss even deeper, plunging her tongue through my lips.

She pulled her hands from my hair and ripped her shirt open. Buttons sprayed and pinged off the floor, but she didn't seem to care. And I sure as hell didn't. I cupped her breasts in my hands. The scant lace provided very little coverage and I could see her dark areolas. Then I slid my palms over her nipples. She loved friction, and I was happy to give her some.

And then she unfastened the front clasp of her bra and slid the shirt and the bra from her shoulders. She pulled back and bit her lip, spread her legs apart and pulled me between them. Her hot flesh scorched mine, making me groan.

When she arched her back so her breast was a focal point

which it usually was- I licked my lips then swirled my tongue around her already hard nipple.

Silas reached from behind her to toy with the other breast then slid half onto the bar beside her so he could take that one into his mouth.

She moaned at the double attention, making blood pound straight to my cock. I didn't know when Viktor joined us, but he was kissing her lips now.

Perfect. I dropped my hand to brush her clit through her pants. She whimpered and pushed closer to my fingers.

There was something exquisite in watching her while she was in the throes of passion. I stood back for a second, still touching her through her pants but watching Viktor kiss her and Silas tease her. She leaned back now, so that Viktor was holding her up with his hand under her head and the other toying with the nipple I'd just stopped sucking.

I wanted to savor this memory, burn it into my mind. If I couldn't find a way to get out of my marriage with Posy, I would need this memory to get me through.

Silas lifted his head and murmured something into her ear, and she laid back on the bar. He flicked open the fly of her pants and she shimmied out of them while still kissing Viktor. But then she turned her head out of his kiss and pulled me in for one.

I pressed my lips against hers and used my tongue to part her lips. Her mouth was hot and wet, and I never wanted to stop kissing her. She slid her hand into my hair, held my head at the back as if I would be the one who pulled away.

The kiss deepened and we both moaned. I couldn't see what the others were doing to her, and I didn't care as I slipped a finger inside her pussy. She was hot and wet, and I wanted to be inside her but I waited, letting my fingers push in, pull out and I watched her. Watched the ecstasy come over her. It was divine. The way her lips parted on a sigh.

The way her hand curled into the front of my shirt as she tried to pull me down.

The way she pushed her chest up and yanked Silas in for the kiss I should've taken.

It was all exquisite.

She gasped and panted and sighed. She arched and moved and breathed. She kissed and clutched and whimpered, every second of it adding to the perfection of these moments.

Viktor had moved to the end of the counter and Erin slid her hips toward him. I took my fingers away and she cried out. I bent her leg and slid my finger back in below, so Viktor could get to her clit with his mouth. He licked and swirled, moved it around and around with the timing of my fingers, then went back to teasing the swollen nub that was her passion button.

She writhed, lifted her hips, did everything she could to make sure the spot she wanted licked was the one he got to. Silas kept his mouth closed around her nipple and she held onto him even as she tried to pull me down for another kiss. "No, sweetheart. I want to watch you."

And I did. More than anything I'd ever wanted. I watched her eyelashes flutter against her cheeks and her hands clench in Silas's hair and against my chest. She twisted my shirt in her fist, and I loved how much strength she put into it. She tugged and pulled, shifted her body and her face pinched. She was close.

The walls of her pussy tightened around my fingers, and I flicked them inside of her, curled them in and out as she rode my hand and Viktor's mouth. She yanked Silas up for a kiss while she moaned and writhed, her pussy squeezing my fingers in a rhythmic dance.

When she finally stopped shivering, she smiled up at me. "Now I want to watch you while I fuck Silas and Viktor takes my ass and I suck your cock."

I loved when she talked dirty. I loved it even more when she told me what she wanted.

She climbed off the bar and sauntered over to my bedroom door. I was only a couple steps behind because oh, God, I wanted this. She choreographed everyone's placement, like last time. I was kneeling in front of her just off to one side, Silas was under her, and Viktor was behind her. She was on her hands and knees.

And then all the light in the world focused on her, or so it seemed in my head as she took my already hard cock into her mouth and sucked deep.

Her mouth was a marvel. A masterpiece. And there weren't words for how incredible it felt to be in her mouth, to have her tongue gliding against my skin while she coaxed my body. I was harder than I'd ever been. More ready than I could've imagined being.

She held herself up with one arm and wrapped the other around my ass, pulling me closer, forcing me deeper into her throat. And I'd never felt anything so incredible in my life.

I groaned and held onto the edge of the headboard behind me for dear life. When I couldn't stand it anymore, when my body was coiled and my mind was spinning, she dug her fingers into my ass cheeks, and she pulled me as deep as I could go in her mouth. I came. So hard.

Shuddering. Gasping. Groaning.
Embarrassingly loudly.

The intensity of the orgasm shook me. Rocked me backward and made my knees weak.

And then they all joined me in bliss. Erin was writhing and moaning. And when she lifted her head, all I could see was the ecstatic smile on her swollen lips.

She was a fantasy vision.

All the problems with my brother, with my family, still existed, still lingered and there was nothing I could do about them. But at this moment, I didn't care. Nothing in the world compared to this week, with these three people. With the friendships. With the care. I couldn't imagine ever finding this with Posy.

Maybe when I was king, I would make them my most trusted advisors. Wouldn't that turn some heads. My mother's would spiral right off her shoulders, but I couldn't bear the idea of never seeing them again.

I couldn't stand the thought of going back to the life I had before.

Maybe, if I didn't go back, my parents would pass me over for Nicky. It was what Nicky wanted. My mother had certainly put the idea in my father's head. And I didn't mind the thought that much. Not nearly as much as I once would have. I didn't want to give my life to service to my country if it meant I could never see these people again.

There had to be a way to work this out. Had to be something I could do. If not, maybe I would call my mother and tell her that Nicky would be a better choice for king. I didn't care anymore.

That would have to be a last resort because news like that, delivered to my mother, might actually kill her.

CHAPTER 17

Silas

Viktor and Erin napped, but I couldn't sleep. So, after Henryk and Ray left the suite, I sat on the sofa watching videos on my phone. I was engrossed in a true-crime story about a woman who'd shot her husband and hid his body in the family freezer for ten years before it was discovered. It was vivid and well-told.

Otherwise, I wouldn't have startled at the knock on the door. After a few seconds, I stood. Certainly no one was at the door who wanted to kill me. But as I swung it open, my opinion on that matter changed.

This had to be Princess Posy. After all the talk yesterday about her, I'd done a quick Google search on her. She was a beauty, there was no denying it, and she smelled like money. Specifically, she smelled like perfume that cost a lot of money.

"Can I help you?" I was polite but on guard. There were plenty of tales about how women scorned exacted their revenge. I had to be cautious.

"So, you're one of the men who shares a woman with my fiancé." She brushed past me as if I'd invited her in. I shut the door and her perfume wafted after her in a big cloud.

Then she spun a full circle in the center of the patio. She was wearing a coral sundress with a big hat and sunglasses that took up half her face. As she whirled, her dress flared and she removed her sunglasses and hat, then tossed them onto the chair.

And then she smiled up at me. "Is Henryk here?"

I shook my head. "No. He's with Ray." The dress made her skin look a deeper tan. She rubbed her arms. I had an urge to start a fire in the fireplace to warm her, but that was silly. It was hot. "Can I help you?"

She looked me up and down, leered, if I was honest, and smiled when she lifted her eyes to my face again. "I imagine a man like you is quite skilled at helping a woman, but I orgasmed in the car on the way over."

Her smile widened. If she'd said it for the shock value, she scored that point. Although, I had to admit, she looked like a woman who knew how to orgasm probably on her own command.

"You're the reason we're all in Spain." I had no reason to speak, no idea why I did, or what the hell I was trying to say when I said it.

"Oh? Do tell?" Her voice was a husky rasp.

"Um, yes, well. When we were all seven, we did a ... ceremony. Promised to be husbands and wife forever. She married all of us." I cleared my throat. I was explaining this so badly, but I didn't really have a choice but to keep going. "And then we were all grown up and minding our business, going about our lives, and we got papers. I think Erin got a phone call, I'm not really sure. We had to come to Lichtenstein to get divorced. Formally."

"And so you all started sleeping together. Makes perfect sense." She smiled but I had a feeling–a strange and disturbing one probably brought on by the video I was watching–that I needed to get between her and her handbag. She'd probably brought a weapon, hid it in the bag and planned to kill us all. She moved closer to me, and I took a step back. "Why is such a big man afraid of such a tiny woman?"

It was true. She wasn't much taller than a kid and not built much bigger. Or maybe it seemed that way because I was so tall. I didn't know, but it was silly for me to be afraid of her.

I smiled because she was right.

"What do you have to drink here?" She moved to stand behind the bar and opened the refrigerator, surveying the contents. She pulled a bottle of beer and twisted off the cap. "Cheers."

I didn't have a drink, so I nodded and smiled. "Cheers."

She pulled another beer and slid it across the counter at me. "Drink. It's going to be a long chat we have."

Her accent wasn't quite British, didn't sound Middle Eastern, wasn't as pronounced as Henryk's and sounded not at all Spanish. I couldn't place it. "Where are you from?"

"Morovia." She smiled and tipped her bottle back again. "And you are American." Her hair bounced along with her nod. "I love Americans. They have no little voices that stop them from doing things."

I had a little voice in my head, but I also knew how to ignore it, or tell it to piss off when I didn't like its message. But I smiled at her. "My little voice has a right to remain silent."

She laughed, and it sounded like a high-pitched little bell. "So I've read."

That was a hit on what the tabloids had reported, and I didn't acknowledge it. Not because my little voice said not to, but because the world would be a much nicer place if we didn't acknowledge every hit. That was my take, anyway.

I smiled at her because I didn't know what else to do. "Henryk has spoken fondly of you." And she lit up, smiled broadly. "Says you're handling the forced marriage much better than he is."

"Obviously." She finished her beer, reached for another. "Henryk has always been a man who knew his own heart." She smiled. "And I was a never a part of that heart." Her shrug was unbothered, and her smile didn't waver. "It's all right. Traditional marriage is not an expectation. Or a promise, even."

I scoffed. "What does that mean?" My confusion was honest, and I didn't mean to sound judgmental.

"It means that I, too, have preferences and Henryk is not one of them. He can have his life and I can have mine." She raised her eyebrows as if she was waiting for me to get clued in. To be honest, I didn't care. "I prefer women."

"Oh." Again, I didn't care.

"My... companion is jealous, but she knows Henryk and I will have a duty to produce an heir. Of course, we already must be discreet, she and I, so that won't be an issue. That's why I've come to speak to Henryk. He needs to know we can work this out, but that we have to make agreements."

It all made sense to me, and Erin would be happy to hear it. And like I'd thought her into wakefulness, she walked into the room. "I'm Erin Wright." She held out her hand to Posy.

Posy gave her the same look she'd given me. "I'm Posy of

Morovia." She cocked an eyebrow. "My sister is Rose, and my mother is Lily." She rolled her eyes and gave a slight but abrupt head shake. "Horrible tradition."

Erin put her hand on my shoulder as she took my bottle of beer and drank. "I heard you make the call earlier. He told me how humiliated you are."

Posy laughed. "My father was standing there. I couldn't very well give Henryk a verbal fist bump when I'm supposed to be the woman scorned." She rolled her eyes. "Royals have been doing this since before Henry the 8th started taking heads." This was a woman who knew her own mind, who had obviously thought about this enough to concoct a plan. "I'm here right now, demanding my future husband be true and faithful to me. Much as I'm promising" –she put up a long-fingered set of air quotes– "to be faithful to him."

"So this is okay with you?" I waved a finger in the air, meaning the suite, the occupants, the incredible sex we'd been having.

"Do I need Henryk to be a faithful husband? It wouldn't be fair to him since I only plan to have enough sex with him to produce an heir." She was aloof and dismissive and haughty, but the woman made a striking figure and she spoke with the appropriate amount of puffed-up overconfidence that I would expect of someone in her position.

But damn, she must've gone to the Meryl Streep school of acting. I couldn't tell whether it was the phone call from before, or this that she was faking.

I shook my head at her. "What about the articles?"

She sighed and leaned forward so that both of her hands were braced on the edge of the bar. "He's going to have to fix that. Probably buy me some nice bauble, publicly proclaim his undying love to me and say that the dalliance here is nothing more than a sowing of his wild oats, then we will work out an arrangement." She took another drink of beer and then straightened. "Now, where is Henryk? We need to work on the article we're going to release to the public."

Erin stared hard at the princess. "Pretty brave of you to tell us about your... dalliances." It might've been just an observation, but it was pointed.

The princess walked out from behind the bar and went to stand in front of Erin, who'd turned to face Posy. "Jealous one, are you?" She smiled and curled her finger under Erin's chin to tilt it up. "Don't worry, little American, I have no designs on Henryk. I wouldn't sleep with him at all if my country didn't require it." And then she moved closer to Erin, so they were almost chest to chest. "I much prefer a woman. Gentle hands, the heat of her mouth, the softness of her body." She held Erin's gaze as she stroked her hands down Erin's sides and brought them back up then leaned in, and I thought–just for a second–that she was going to kiss Erin, but at just the moment their mouths should've met, Posy pulled back. "You can have him. I only need his sperm."

Holy shit.

And Posy continued even after she'd stepped away. "Henryk can have his wild weekend with you all, parade you through the streets of Ibiza if he so desires. But come Monday, he needs to be home, diligently in front of the cameras and our families planning a wedding. Contrite. And if he cannot bear to be without you until our marriage license is posted, then..." She shrugged. "I don't care. He can have you all. But in front of the world, he is mine and I am his."

Her tone brokered no room for negotiation. Not that I was

interested in negotiating with her. And Erin didn't have a reason to try. "If he needs a wife so badly, why can't Henryk just marry Erin?"

Posy shrugged as though her answer made perfect sense. "Because she's not the princess of America, and I don't want to have to marry the child, Nickolai."

And I supposed in a strange way, it did make sense.

Posy walked to the table, and she had a walk that begged watching. But I wasn't attracted. She was too thin, too... regal. I could see her in a full crown and gown. But then she opened her bag, pulled out a stack of cards, sat at the table and started shuffling.

Her long fingers maneuvered the cards like she dealt poker at a casino, and I watched for a minute. No fucking way was I betting money with someone who could handle a deck like that. That came from years of practice. So, either she was a sleight of hand magician, or she had mad card shark skills. I wasn't taking any chances with either.

Her glance from below her lowered lashes was pure come hither. This was a woman who knew how to use her sexuality. It would've been more convincing had she not just told me she preferred women. "Come, let's play cards."

She had one of those wicked grins, and I laughed and shook my head. "No, no. I don't have big stakes money to lose to you, Princess Posy." I liked saying her name with her title. It sounded more playful than as if I was actually addressing royalty. And it made the princess smile too.

"I love American irreverence." She laughed and waved me over. "Come on. Play. we won't bet money. We can play strip poker."

I had no doubt I would be naked by the end of the first hand, and I shook my head, ready to decline.

But Erin smiled. "I'll play."

She'd had a rough couple of days. And if she wanted to blow off steam playing cards with the princess, I wasn't going to let her play alone. "Fine. Deal me in."

It was the least I could do.

CHAPTER 18

Erin

We'd been playing cards for a couple hands–Silas only had his boxers left to lose and he would be naked–when Viktor walked out of the bedroom, adorably rumpled from sleep and rubbing his eyes.

He looked at Silas and shook his head. "You better not have bet my money."

Silas, ever the good sport, grinned. "Do I look like I've been betting money?" And he had a sense of humor. I liked that about him so much.

Posy looked at Viktor, then at me. "Well, you do attract the large, brawny ones, don't you?"

I shrugged. "We were seven when we met. I just got lucky this is how they grew up." Could've been models or mountain men. It didn't matter to me. That they took care of themselves made them more attractive.

Viktor walked closer. He'd showered and smelled clean and

fresh. He pulled out the chair between me and Posy and opposite Silas.

He reached across the table to shake hands with the princess. "I'm Viktor."

She smiled. "I'm Posy, Princess of Morovia."

"Of course." He shrugged at me. "I guess I should've known that."

I was more interested in ferreting out information from the chattier by the moment princess. "How long have you known Henryk?"

"There are pictures of us in the bath together as toddlers. Ran in every newspaper in each of our countries." She rolled her eyes. "His penis didn't get near the attention back then."

This was the story that was going to haunt Henryk for a while, anyway. "Well, it's worthy of attention now."

She laughed and the sound was genuine. "Apparently." And then she looked at me. "We didn't meet again after until I was ten and he was twelve." She laughed just a little bit. "I knew when I didn't find such a handsome boy even remotely attractive that I was different. Although I did try. He was my first kiss. My first... time."

"You had sex with him?" I wasn't jealous as much as curious. Maybe a little jealous.

"We were bumbling teenagers." She laid her cards face down on the table. "I assume he has better technique now, but back then we had no idea. And I was still trying to discover who I was and hide my inner self at the same time. It was a horrible time for both of us." We'd stopped playing to chat and she chuckled. "Nicky was acting out, partying like a twenty-five-year-old at the tender age of thirteen. The family buried as many of the stories as they could. Had to buy a newspaper to keep Nicky's affair out of it."

"Affair?" This might've been information Henryk could use to keep the little brother in line. I hated that I'd even had the thought, but Nicky started playing dirty first.

Posy nodded. "He and one of the teachers at his school...a librarian, I think. It was torrid. Went on for months. He had pictures and messages between them. And he was blackmailing her over it."

"Did Henryk know?" If he didn't know, I wasn't going to be the one who told him.

"Of course, he knew. We all knew what was happening. Both royal families. And when it all blew up, Nicky went to 'rehab' and the teacher went away." She wagged her finger across the table at me. "I can see your American mind working. But this can never come out. Henryk won't let it."

"Why not?" Certainly, Nicky had to know he couldn't just act out at his own will without facing the consequences. And if there was justice in the world, Henryk and I would get to choose the consequences.

"Henryk is a proper older brother. He's protective. And despite the fact that Nicky is spoiled and doesn't appreciate it, he won't let Nicky get hurt." She spoke so confidently, but she hadn't been with us the last few days. She had no idea what Nicky was putting us through. I'd lost my promotion because of that spoiled, selfish brat.

"Henryk is considering giving up the crown because of him. I lost my–"

"He's *what*?" Her voice went shrill and loud. She was all cool and calm until it was her future in that little turd's hands. "He can't give up the throne. That would be... insanity." She shook her head and held up her hand. "I'm not marrying that little jerk."

I didn't know if it was my place to tell her or not, but that's what I did. "It's because Nicky is the one feeding stories to the papers. If it doesn't stop, his mother and father have both said that they'll make Nicky the heir and Henryk said he isn't certain that it's a bad idea." That was the gist of it, anyway.

"Can I ask you a question?" Silas looked at her, eyebrow cocked. When she nodded, he continued, "Why don't you just come out as gay? Is it against your country's religion?"

She shrugged. "It wouldn't matter. In my position, we marry for convenience. For alliance. For betterment of our countries. We don't have choices."

I understood the obligations, the reasons to lie and hide parts of themselves, particularly it became clear in the last couple days.

Posy looked at me, her gaze hard. "Henryk and I could come to an understanding. We would have to, but you all would have to agree, too. Would have to learn discretion."

We knew discretion. We knew how to keep the details tight and quiet. "We're dealing with a tabloid reporter."

She scoffed and shook her head. "We're always dealing with tabloid reporters. Henryk is not unique in that."

Of course, I knew she was right. But there also must be a way to get around them. "How do you deal with them?"

She shrugged. "I think I've been lucky. I'm not a gorgeous prince. Women buy those magazines five times more than men. My face on one isn't as valuable as his."

I didn't know the statistics or if she had the figures correct, but it didn't really matter either. I wasn't going to argue the numbers or the logic. I nodded instead. And it did make sense.

She glanced at Silas then Viktor. "He could pop you into his staff. No one would think twice. But your face is out there now, and for a few years, it's going to be everywhere. Anytime you show up the same place he does, on a flight to anywhere that connects to Lichtenstein. Until the sensationalism of the story dies, *you* are the story." She pointed a long, manicured nail in my direction. "Whether you're banging him or not."

Oh, good. That was something to look forward to.

"Once they can't link you with him, they'll move on." This one knew how to use a cocked eyebrow and a dramatic pause. "Eventually."

I nodded because there wasn't much else I could do.

"What if she doesn't go back to her life?"

Posy shrugged. "Then *she'll* have to get thicker skin." She'd been through this a time or two. "For those reporters this is a job. Probably not even the job they want, but it isn't personal. You have to remember that." She shot me a pointed look.

Oh, yeah. I would so remember that while they were ruining my life and my career and my job prospects.

When Henryk walked in the door, he stopped, stared and then walked a couple more steps into the room. "Posy. What are you...?"

"Arriving, ready to whirl you around town, show you off, make the world believe that there isn't trouble in paradise and that we're all friends now." She sighed as if it was a big trial to be around him. I didn't know the exact extent of their relationship, but I would bet they would make an interesting king and queen.

"Maybe you should go get married right now." Silas cocked his head as if just now considering the idea–after he'd spoken it. Then he nodded. "Yeah. It couldn't hurt."

Henryk frowned and shook his head. "My mother would kill me. I can't deny her a royal wedding."

I nodded. I'd watched two royal weddings–one in real time, one on video from years and years ago–and the splendor was undeniable. As was the merchandise sales.

So I would have to watch Henryk marry her and there was nothing I could do about it. I sighed inwardly and outwardly kept a smile plastered on my face. But next to me, Viktor nudged my shoulder. "You look constipated." His whisper warmed the shell of my ear, and I tilted my head toward the heat of his mouth. He laid his arm over the back of my chair and toyed with my hair as Ray came closer.

Silas had claimed his clothes back from the pile Posy and I had accumulated, and I smiled as he sat next to me on the opposite side.

Ray leaned on the back of an empty chair. "Henryk has been trying to get hold of you. To explain."

"I saw the pictures, Raymond." She looked at me. "He's so professional." Then to Ray she said, "I think the pictures said everything he needed to say."

"Maybe Silas is right," I said quietly. I didn't want Henryk to get married. But if the world thought I was merely a dalliance he'd gotten out of his system, maybe they would leave me alone. "Maybe you should get married."

"My mother..."

I shook my head. "I don't mean run away and elope." Although that would send a pretty clear message to the tabloids. "I mean move up the date. Publicly plan the whole thing."

Henryk looked at Posy. "Harlow was unkind." To me he said, "But I've spoken to her. Hired her as the"–he cleared his throat and tried not to look at Ray while clearing looking at Ray– "Royal Recorder."

Ray's eyebrows disappeared into his hairline. "You did *what*?"

"I didn't have a choice. She was going to run the story about four little seven-year-olds in a public park in Washington DC marrying each other. She was going to turn a child's game into an international incident. My Mother's head would've exploded." Henryk shook his head, but he was smiling.

I didn't know which part he found more amusing, but I liked that he was working around the anger to find humor in it.

Ray chuckled and shook his head at Henryk. "And you think this will keep her skull attached?" He obviously had more of a relationship with Henryk than employer/employee. "The messes you get yourself into..."

Henryk frowned and I wished I could figure out how to make this better for all of us, but right now, I couldn't figure out how to handle my own problems. I had to figure out what I was going to do about a job.

I didn't want to walk back into Joffrey Vandeloo's office with everyone I'd worked with knowing I'd been passed over for the promotion because of my social life. My 9-5 was their business. Outside of that, no one had the right to judge me, but that fucking reporter had taken my private life public, and chances were, I wasn't going to make it back from it.

Certainly, it would be difficult for me to be taken seriously. My career–all those years of school, the student loans–was worthless now. Who was going to trust me to sell their product?

Depression sank over me, and I didn't care what they were talking about anymore. I needed a minute.

CHAPTER 19

Viktor

Oh, what it must've been like to be a prince who was obviously kissed by the gods. He was good-looking. Had money. Could up and leave and pay for a vacation at his leisure.

I was jealous, but who wouldn't have been? He had it all. And so what if the world knew what he did in his bedroom? To my way of thinking, this was a whole lot of big deal about nothing. Who he had sex with didn't have anything to do with how fit he was to run a country. Sex was sex. Matters of government were matters of government. Neither had anything to do with the other.

"I can't sleep with someone and be married to you." Henryk stared at his fiancée. She was gorgeous. How lucky could a guy get to be married to her and have Erin?

"What?" Erin sat forward and twisted to look at him around me. "She said..."

"It doesn't matter what she said. I can't do it. I'm not ..." He shook his head and grimaced. "I would never do that to her."

Posy laughed. "You won't be doing anything *to* me." It took a second, but finally Henryk smiled.

He murmured a semi-polite response then added, "I have to provide an heir." So, he would be sleeping with her too. As if I needed more proof he led a charmed life.

She laughed. "I have a turkey baster."

The conversation was devolving, and if I were honest, I was dead tired of hearing about it.

The woman he was supposed to marry had come to Ibiza just to tell him he could do as he damned well pleased so long as he kept it quiet. If I lived to be a hundred, wasn't likely I would ever meet someone so lucky.

I pushed my chair back and stood. Erin glanced up, and I shot her a wink. Hopefully, she didn't find it as smarmy as it felt, but I needed a minute. I had to get out of there before I said something I couldn't take back. Before I reminded Henryk that prince or not, he was a grown man, capable of making a fucking decision about his own life.

Maybe it was different for princes. I couldn't comment on that part because I didn't know anything about his situation, but I could say that if he didn't start putting his foot down, he was going to be a king without a kingdom. Someone would sense his weakness, come in and claim the kingdom for himself, steal it, likely while Henryk was still waiting for permission to fight.

I walked outside, stood at the railing and stared out at the rolling waves. It was beautiful here, there was no doubt. The water was clear, and the whitecaps looked like they'd been painted on. And the sky was so blue that if I turned just right, it was hard to tell where the water ended, and the sky began. The breeze was light and warm enough to ruffle my hair, but not blow me back.

This was a perfect night, except for the drama. I could've happily lived without that.

I loved it here, but if I had to go home, it didn't matter as long as I had Silas and Erin and even the prince.

It didn't look like we were in a situation that was going to work, though. I could feel it all coming to an end whenever I looked at any of them. And the regret ached through me.

Silas walked out of the suite to the patio and stood beside me, handed me a beer then knocked the bottom of his against the bottom of mine. "Glad I'm not a prince," he said, his usual smile in place.

This was a guy who found the good in life and hung onto it. Found reasons to smile even when he had to hunt for the good. He was a good friend.

"So what did I miss?" I wasn't sure how much I cared, but I'd asked so it all must've meant something to me.

He shrugged. "Princess Posy told Henryk that he can have all the threesomes, foursomes, fivesomes— whatever he wants."

I had been in there for that part. I nodded, even though the information wasn't new. "Erin said she isn't going to be able to choose between us all, so she hopes she doesn't have to."

He shook his head. "I hope she doesn't have to." I agreed on this point. "I'm not going to make her choose. After all the women we've shared, we're brothers now." I felt the same way.

There was a slight humming sound, like a giant fly or a really aggressive bumblebee, and since I couldn't see or distinguish where the sound was coming from, I ignored it at first, continuing talking to Silas, but it seemed to be getting louder, moving closer. I looked up. Saw it. My jaw clenched because this was getting out of hand, and I was past pissed off.

"Are you fucking kidding me?" Silas was on his feet, trying to grab the drone that was toying with us now. Coming closer. Flying up. Moving in again. Drifting away.

I didn't know if it meant his brother was in Ibiza, but if this was Nickolai's handiwork, and right then, there was no reason to believe otherwise, he was going to answer for what he'd done to all of us.

I wasn't worried that the damned thing was still here, but I had no idea how much it had heard when I'd first noticed the buzzing sound. We'd been talking about our relationship. Private details.

At this point, the stories about Erin and Henryk made it all look so sordid. Silas and I—from the initial pictures, anyway—were nothing more than observers. But if that fucking drone had heard even a part of our conversation, the next article would damn us all. Even Posy.

Someone needed to go inside and warn them. I opened the door to the suite and walked in quietly, listening to the conversation. They were still discussing the wedding, the articles, the drone.

"There's another one." I hadn't meant to interrupt or blurt it, but I did.

Erin whipped her head toward me. "Another one? Another drone?" Her voice was shrill, and I went to her, laid a hand on her shoulder. I wanted to comfort her, to infuse her with the knowledge I wouldn't let this happen to her again.

But I nodded and she shook her head. She didn't need comfort, she was angry. She slammed her hand on the table in front of her. The beer bottles clanged and the wine glass that had whiskey in it shifted, but nothing toppled.

"I'm going to kill him." She meant Nickolai, and I couldn't blame her. "That little shit isn't going to have to worry about being king." Her tone was hard, and I didn't doubt her intent or her ability. "It's going to be hard to sit on a throne with my foot up his ass."

My lips twitched with a smile I held back, but Henryk frowned. "We don't know that this one is one of his or one that belongs to Lichtenstein."

Silas walked inside, holding the offending drone in one hand. "I'm certain that it is."

He held it up. A seal of the Royal Army of Lichtenstein was painted on the bottom. "Is that evidence enough for you, Fancy... Henryk?" Silas asked, his voice softer but deep with anger too. I'd known him long enough to be able to read him. Pissed off, on Silas, was a tense face, muscles in his jaw hard, teeth clenched.

Henryk sighed loud and long, like he'd been holding it in a while and had just now decided to let it go. "It isn't that big of a deal anymore."

"What?" I had to hear the logic behind this one. Yesterday, it was the biggest deal in all the land.

"The stories are already out there. They might add a new detail or two, but the damage is done." He sounded more resigned to it than accepting of it. "And it will all be forgotten once Posy and I drown them all in wedding details."

I glanced at Erin. She looked away. Only one of them was resigned and accepting. Erin was pissed, although she wore it well. Even narrow-eyed and her normally full lips thin and compressed, she was beautiful.

"No." Her voice was quiet at first. "No." Then louder. "*No.*" And now everyone was looking at her.

"I don't have a choice."

Henryk took resigned to a whole other level. He added a head-shake, downcast eyes, and another sigh. "Everyone has a choice."

She shook her head.

Henryk stared at her. "Is that your American bumper sticker logic?" When she tilted her head and her eyes flashed, he looked away. "I'm sorry. I didn't mean that." The silence in the room stretched over us. "I've talked to everyone I know, everyone I can think of who might possibly know what to do, and there is nothing else I can do. I'm going back and marrying Posy."

He sounded as though he was being led to the gallows and Posy laughed. "I'll try not to be insulted by your tone."

He sighed again and looked at her. "I'm sorry."

She held up her hand. "Don't worry. I get it."

But Erin hadn't really stopped shaking her head and she looked at them both. "There has to be another way."

He gazed at her. "Not without shaming my crown and hurting my parents." He raked a hand through his hair and then shook his head until it laid back in its place. "I can't do that. Even for you."

He said it as though if there was anyone he would do it for, it would be Erin. And that was a sentiment I understood. Whole-heartedly.

CHAPTER 20

Erin

The night was long and sleepless because I couldn't stop trying to think of ways to get around all of this. I ran through about a hundred different scenarios, but I didn't know enough about Lichtenstein or the royal family there to be able to be much help.

So I wasted the night contemplating things that I couldn't possibly do anything about. And if there was a thing that would make a girl feel useless, it was that.

By breakfast, I was in a mood. Someone had ordered food and there was a vat of eggs and bacon on the table with golden, buttery croissants and a stack of pancakes that, though tall, probably wouldn't last long enough for Henryk to wake up.

I searched the headlines on my phone, and of course, there was another article, another batch of them. Someone had provided details of our "wedding" more than a decade ago. The memories, as I read, came in vivid flashes of standing with Silas and Viktor and Henryk as we all promised to be best friends for as long as we lived, and to never forget how important we all were to each other. We were seven, so we didn't speak so eloquently and I couldn't remember the exact words, but I could remember everything else. All the other details.

Henryk had been in a white shirt with khaki shorts. I'd been wearing my Oshkosh B'Gosh overalls also in a white shirt, but mine had tiny little unicorns and rainbows all over it. Silas was wearing jeans shorts and a red shirt that had the Superman emblem on the front. And Viktor was all in blue–dark blue shorts and a light blue shirt with blue sneakers. We'd stood in a circle, held hands, made our promises then went back to playing at the playground.

It was funny how vivid the pictures were in my mind.

Back then, forever hadn't meant much. I didn't have the concept of time back then. And to be honest, until I'd gotten the phone call from Henryk, I hadn't remembered that day. But once he called, it all came back to me. And after the last week and a half, I wasn't going off into the night, back to my old life without them. All of them.

I'd called Posy before I came out for breakfast, and she breezed in as only she could. She laid her sweater on the back of the sofa then walked to the table and smiled.

"So, is this the big goodbye scene?" She puffed out her lower lip as she glanced at Silas and Viktor then at me. To her, all the gloominess probably seemed silly, but to me, it was a devastating reality. She stared for a second at each one of us then shook her head. "My goodness. You all look like someone kicked your puppies."

That was a pretty accurate description of how I felt and how the others looked, so I didn't argue.

She held up her phone and gave it a little wave. Whatever she wanted us to see, she didn't want us to see very well, or she was going to tell anyway, so it didn't matter. "The tabloids have documented my angry outburst after my visit to the Ibiza love nest of the prince and his sexual partners. I apparently have demanded that you all leave the resort and stay away from Henryk. And I've gone so far as to threaten legal action against the Royal Crown of Lichtenstein. I'm apparently an angry shrew of a woman." She laughed and gave a slight head shake. "These papers have such a way with the truth."

"A wicked way," Silas corrected. "Sad, right?"

Posy shook her head and shrugged. "I've learned to deal with it. Whenever I ventured out of the castle, someone printed a story. I went to a friend's baby shower once and the papers printed that it was to celebrate my *secret* love child with the head of my security staff."

She might've learned to let it all roll off her back, but I wasn't so forgiving. "Don't you get mad?" I was ready to throw down, go full-on lady wrestler. And not because they'd lied. What they done was imply but hadn't written an outright lie about me. It was the invasion of my privacy, the violation of what was acceptable decorum.

"The people who know me know the truth." I wished I had her confidence. "*You* know the truth about you, and a few broken hearts in your wake isn't a crime or a sin or whatever you think the rest of the world thinks. What does it matter what a bunch of strangers think about you?" For my part, the articles had cost me a promotion, but I wasn't about to whine about that to someone who was so well put-together and probably already thought I was making a mountain out of an anthill.

She looked at me then at Silas and Viktor and Henryk. "He has to care." She jerked a thumb at Henryk. "But you have a freedom he doesn't."

"If he's going to be king, he can change how things are." Even after I'd spoken the words, I thought how ridiculous it was that he was so bound by his position and his happiness meant nothing to the world. But I cared about his happiness.

Posy looked at me. "You're all living the life you want to live." And then she smiled a perfect, white-toothed smile. She was pretty in a way women were in magazines. She was tall and thin, lithe with dark hair and dark eyes, so dark they looked as if the pupil had overtaken all the other color. And she dressed like she had her own personal shopper who had clothes specifically designed for her. Every garment fit like a glove. "I envy you all. Don't let them make you have to apologize or hide your face. You know your happiness."

It was easy to say that I wouldn't apologize. Easy to think I could stand up to the scrutiny and the gossip and story after story of innuendo and name calling. I wanted to. More than I'd ever wanted anything, I wanted to be loud and proud about the relationship I was in with Silas, Viktor, and Henryk. But that would only feed the ghost. Would only make it louder. And it would make it harder for Henryk. I didn't want that.

But I nodded at Posy because she was being supportive. Being a good person. And I wanted to model myself after her. To be admirable, tough enough to let it roll off my back, but I wasn't feeling it. And that wasn't like me. I had been through a lot in my life. This wasn't going to be the thing that took me down.

I lifted my head, renewed. Refreshed. Resolved. And whatever was coming for me, whatever person they sent to attempt to take me down, they had some work to do. Because I was formidable. A badass. And I deserved my happiness. No one was taking that away from me.

Before I could proclaim my new lease on life, Henryk looked at me and I was lost in his face. He sighed. "I have never had a week like this before. Never felt so content and peaceful even when the day was anything but." His smile warmed me. "But I can't be a part of this anymore. I can't marry a woman and be unfaithful. Not even for you." This time when he looked at me, it was as if he was trying not to see me. "But that I can't doesn't mean you shouldn't be together. You should go on and know that it's what I want for you."

He looked at me, smiled, even nodded, but I couldn't be with Silas and Viktor and not with Henryk. I hoped he knew that.

I shook my head. For a minute, I couldn't speak. I couldn't think. I couldn't let this end. There were too many emotions. Anger. Grief as if I was losing someone, and I couldn't let that happen.

"No. Just no." I shook my head. I couldn't let go. I would not. "Tomorrow, we're all going back to Lichtenstein. Tomorrow." Time had passed so quickly. "Wow." I shook off the wonder because it wouldn't help us. We needed a plan. A way to stay together. "What we have is good. It's friendship. It's care. And you know..." I looked from one of them to another. "It's really good sex." I hoped Posy found this kind of happiness. And I was going to fight for mine.

"Erin, my obligations are very different."

"And you walked into this knowing you had those obligations." We had bribed him into coming along, but I didn't care about the logistics of it all. "I can't give up without trying."

He glanced at me. "No one's fought for me before."

"I'm sorry for that, but I'm fighting now."

Henryk's head tilted as he gazed at me. "You haven't met the queen yet."

"Your mother?" When he nodded, I smiled. "Well, don't get the rings just yet because the queen hasn't met me, either."

And things were about to get really interesting.

THE END

* * *

The final story is available for pre-order now:
https://books2read.com/u/bQj5le